MW01267956

Scandalous

A Novel by

Torrian Ferguson

Copyright © 2005 by Torrian Ferguson

Published by Two of a Kind Publishing
3120 Milton Road
Charlotte, NC 28215

www.twoofakindpublishing.com

All rights reserved. No part of this book may be reproduced or transmitted in any form or by any means, electronic or mechanical, including photocopying, recording, or by any information storage and retrieval system without the written permission from the publisher or author, except for the inclusion of brief quotations in a review.

This is a work of fiction. It is not meant to depict, portray or represent any particular real persons. All the characters, incidents and dialogues are the products of the author's imagination and are not to be constructed as real. Any resemblance to actual events or person living or dead is purely coincidental.

Editor: Danielle Buckery

Book Layout: Lisa Gibson-Wilson
Renaissance Management Services
www.renmanserv.com

Cover Design: www.mariondesigns.com

First printing January 2006

Printed in the United States of America

ISBN: 0-9752589-1-5

Acknowledgements

First and foremost I would like to thank God
for giving me the ability to write.
Without Him none of my books
would have ever made it out of my head.

Secondly I would like to thank my wife and kids.
You all have been very patient with me
while writing and I really appreciate it.
Your love and support keeps me motivated.

Third I would like to thank Lisa Gibson Wilson.
I can never say thank you enough
for all the things you've taught me.
You're more than my literary consultant,
I consider you my friend.

To Estella, Allan, Marsha and Fontella.
Thank you for your unwavering support.
And see, now you can say your names
are in one of my books.
See mama it's not even on a "dirty" page.

Thanks to everyone that has supported me.
I really appreciate all of you.

Thank You.

Author website:
www.torrianferguson.com

CHAPTER 1

Michelle

"Damn Wanda! That's the third hand you've lost in a row. Poker just ain't your game huh?"

My mother has always been a big gambler, but as of late she's been in a slump, a real bad slump. I watched her on several occasions lose our rent money, light money and water bill money. I even had to go to a friend's house and eat a few times 'cause she lost our grocery money too. But the one thing she did that I never understood was, for some strange reason she always played with the biggest ballers in the projects. These were the type of guys that didn't want to wait till you got your check for a payment; they wanted their money on the spot. Most of these guys had to be every bit of forty, forty-five years old. I remember hearing one of them say that the only reason they liked playing cards with Mama was because she gave good head when she couldn't pay. But recently, when ever I heard Mama slam her cards to the table I knew what I had to do.

"Wanda how you gonna pay me this time? I got all your money and what little cheap jewelry you had. And, I'm tired of fuckin' you for payment. What else you got?"

"Michelle, come here!" I knew what she wanted. I was use to it. I was already ready.

"Send him back here Ma!"

I would stand in the doorway just so I could see the guy before he got to my bedroom. The smell of cheap stank ass cologne would fill the hallway leading to my room. I used to get sick to my stomach these fake ass pimps made their way to my room. But after a while I became immune to the smell of Mad Dog 20/20 and English Leather. I just wanted it to be over really soon. I would try and sound really tough when I talked to the guys.

"Unzip your pants!"

I'd drop to my knees and begin performing oral sex on the guy to cover Mama's payment. Some of them would try and hold my head or pull my hair but I wasn't having any of that. One guy even tried to force himself on me but the other people in the house came running when they heard me screaming. Ain't that something, they'll come running if I'm about to get raped but they don't say a word when I'm sucking them off. I must admit I had got pretty good at giving head and actually took a little pride in getting grown men off really fast. A lot of them said the same thing after they came.

"For a teenager, you suck the hell out a dick."

Every so often the thoughts of my childhood just pop into my head. I try not to think about it but it has a lot to do with why I'm the way I am today. But today is a better day. I'm headed north to Bell University in Greenville, North Carolina. It's 644 miles from Orlando, Florida and my mother's house. I couldn't wait till summer was over. I wanted out of her house so bad. After all I had been through growing up, Orlando was one place I had no desire to return to for any reason. Millions of people go to Orlando each year for the amusement parks. I could give less than a damn about all of that. The bus ride to North Carolina was a long one. 21 hours to be exact. The reason it takes so long is because the damn bus stops in every little town between here and there. If the trip takes 21 hours by bus then in a car the trip would only take 10 and a half hours. I met some interesting people on board too. This guy got on the bus in Darien, Georgia. It was about 2:45 A.M. He was tall about 6'4 and slender with that hard thug look. He looked at me and since I had an empty seat next to me I motioned him over. He sat down and instantly started talking to me.

"Hey, so what's your name?"

"Michelle. And you are?"

"Craig. Where are you going?"

"Greenville, North Carolina."

"I'm going to Savannah."

"So you're not gonna be on the bus long then huh?"

Craig is so damn fine. I love those thug looking brothas. Since he was only on the bus for a few hours I had to make a move and quick. The urge came over me to see if I could get with this brotha on the bus. He looked like the type that would be down for almost anything. Besides I caught him taking peaks at my girls: my 42dd breast.

"So, you have a girl?"

"Nah. I have a friend."

"That means, yeah I have a girl but she don't know that I mess around on her."

"So, can you and I be friends till you get off the bus?"

"Damn! You're straight to the point huh?"

"Yeah, no sense in wasting time."

"I feel you. What you feel like doin?"

I reached my hand into the crotch of his pants. I could feel him getting harder and harder by the second. I unzipped his pants and pulled his massive dick through the hole in his boxers. I looked around to make sure no one was looking and ducked my head out of view. He leaned back in the seat as my head bounced up and down in his lap. I tried not to make any loud slurping noises and he tried not to moan too loud. I was a little uncomfortable. Being 5'8, 180lbs is a lot to squeeze into such a small place. But I was on a mission to see how fast I could make him cum. I used every trick I knew to get this guy off. I nibbled on the underside of it. I ran my tongue along the main vein in it. I even flicked my tongue really fast on the head. The guy sitting across from us looked up and damn near fell out his seat. He didn't say a word but he watched the entire time. That was even more exciting. Sucking dick on a bus with an audience. Craig was either holding back or gay as hell, and didn't like the feel of a woman's mouth. My jaws were beginning to hurt. It was taking forever to get him off. I thought, "Damn am I losing my touch or what?" Finally after what seemed like forever. I felt his body start to tense up a little I knew it was just a matter of time before he came.

"I want to cum in your mouth"

That was the one thing I didn't do. Don't cum on my face, my mouth, and you better not get that shit in my hair.

As soon as I felt his breath stop for a second I pulled away and let him cum all over himself.

"Why you didn't catch it!"

"Nigga I ain't your girl! That's some shit your girlfriend do."

He went into the bathroom on the bus and I guess tried to clean himself up. I moved my seat to the front of the bus right behind the driver just in case he came out and wanted to start with me. About an hour later the bus pulled into the Savannah Bus Station. I played like I was sleep. Craig walked right past me and without saying a word and got off the bus. I looked up and saw him hugging some girl.

"Nigga's ain't shit!"

Once the bus pulled off again my mind fell back on Bell University. I was in my junior year and was looking forward to having my own off campus rental house. The house was in a great neighborhood. My friend Eric had signed up to live there also. The school had purchased old homes near the school and turned them into housing for upper classmen. It was only three to a house. It was already furnished with everything you could need. I heard that we would be having another roommate. I hope this person's cool. I don't need some stuck up silly ass to deal with for a year.

I went back to my seat in the rear so I could stretch out and get some sleep. As I was getting comfortable I noticed the guy that had watched me earlier, across from me, staring and rubbing his crotch. Of course the nympho in me started to come out. I slipped off the red thong that I had on under my mini skirt and threw it in his face. He started to inhale my womanly scent and licked the seat of my panties. That almost made me cum on the spot. He slid over to my seat and wanted to start making small talk. I stopped him before he could even say my name is…

"Nigga, I don't want to know your name, your mama name, or where you are from. I'm just in the mood to get mine." He pulled my breast out of my shirt and started nibbling on my nipple. I reached for his dick, and I swear he was so wide I couldn't get my hands around it. That turned me on even more. I had to have it inside me. I looked around the bus to see what other people were doing. It was only four passengers left besides the two of us, and luckily they were sitting close to the front. I made him lay back in the seat and I straddled him backwards.

"Do you want me to put a condom on?" He asked.

"No, just don't cum in me. I hate those things." I know the thrill of me going raw is going to catch up with me someday, but I have been clean so far. I get tested for HIV and other STDs every 6 months. Birth control is also covered. I started using the new patch about three years ago. I pulled my skirt up around my waist. And grabbed his dick to make sure I slid down right on top of it. He grabbed my butt cheeks as I bounced up and down on top of him. I tried to be as quiet as possible but the squishing sounds of my pussy were getting louder and louder. I looked up and saw that the driver of the bus was watching me. I just knew he was going to put us off the bus. He raised his head a little and I saw that he had a smile from ear to ear. I grabbed my breast and licked one of my nipples as the driver watched me. He just laughed a little and kept driving. I turned my attention back to trying to get mine. I felt this guy's dick start to throb.

"I know you're not about to cum!"

"You got some bomb pussy boo. I can't hold it."

I jumped off and let him cover himself with his own nasty cum. I pulled my skirt down and sat across from him.

"Why you move boo?"

"I told you, I don't want to talk to you or get to know you. Besides you have pissed me off anyway, speedy."

"Why it gotta be all that!"

"Nigga please, don't talk to me for the rest of the trip. As a matter of fact don't look at me either."

A few hours later he got off the bus.

"Bye speedy!"

He just turned and gave me a nasty look and left. I hate a man that comes too fast. I laid back across the seats. Only 10 hours to go. Damn I can't wait to get off this bus.

CHAPTER 2

Eric

It's a shame when your parents don't want to be seen with you out in public but it cut to the core when you're going into your senior year in college and they won't even help you move into your house.

"Mama, ya'll ain't coming to help me move in?"

"Eric you know damn well, we're not going down there to that college, for you to embarrass us."

"How do I embarrass ya'll?"

"Boy look at you. You're prettier than half the women on campus. Hell if you weren't mine, I'd think you were some damn beauty queen. Prancing around. You wear more make-up than I do."

That's okay I'm way pass my feelings being hurt by them. It would really mess her up if she knew that the reason I'm like this is because of her brother Dennis. My uncle Dennis started messing with me when I was a little boy. He always told me that the way he touched me was the way a person that really love you touches you. Hell I was with him so many times I thought that men were supposed to be together and everybody else was just wrong and nasty. I was well into my teens when I found out what we were doing was wrong but it was too late then. I was addicted to men. But for some strange reason I still found women attractive at the same time. I was confused from the beginning.

I've driven this road a hundred times before by myself, and this time is not any different. All I can think about is my girl Michelle. She and I have been down since her freshmen year. That girl loves to party and so do I. I remember this one time at the club I met this fine nigga named Gerald. He was one of them down low brothas. He wanted to get with me but didn't want to make it obvious. I watched him as he danced with what looked like twenty different women. But, his eyes always seemed to find me. I moved from one side of the club to the other and he found me every time. I went to the bar and ordered my drink.

"I'll pay for that." I turned and he was standing next to me. He just laid the money in front of me so the bartender didn't know he was paying for the drink. This guy was fine. He was 5-11, 175 lbs of sexy ass man. He looked like he worked out a few times a week. Those thick arms were driving me crazy. I reached in my pocket and pulled out an old business card. I wrote: meet me across the street in 3 minutes. I quickly gulped down my drink and headed for the door. Across the street was a small dark alley. The only thing in the alley was an old dumpster. Once outside I went to the entrance way to the alley to see if Gerald would come outside. Sure enough a few minuets after I walked out he was coming out the door. He saw where I was standing and started walking across the street. I ducked into the alley as he got closer to me. Gerald entered the alley, where I met him with my tongue diving into his mouth. We kissed like old lovers.

"What's your name? I'm Eric."

"Gerald. My name is Gerald."

Our voices were trembling with lust. It was hard to understand what we were saying to each other.

"Gerald, we are going to have to make this a quickie. My girl is inside the club and she's gonna trip if I'm gone too long."

"Not a problem."

We both unzipped our pants and I leaned up against the empty dumpster. He got behind me and I felt his hard thick dick press against my butt cheeks. I was instantly turned on. I reached back and stroked him a little to make sure he was good and hard. He grabbed my hips and with one swift motion he was half way in my ass.

"Damn Gerald, take it easy. It's been a while."

"My bad. I'm just so damn horny. I need to get this ass."

I leaned over a little more so he could go in deeper. He started out slow. I love it when a man knows how to fuck. All of a sudden his pace quickened. I was getting pounded by my new lover. I could feel his balls slap against my upper thighs. That's the best feeling in the world when you feel those balls slapping against you.

"Fuck this ass nigga!"

I was out of control. I felt filled to the brim. I grabbed my dick and started jacking off. I was hard enough to break a rock. With every thrust he went deeper and deeper. Finally I had all of him in me. He leaned forward and began to kiss my neck. The scent of his cologne was all over me. I just stayed there bent over and allowed him to have his way. Without notice I felt shot after shot of hot cum race into my body. I remember thinking, No this nigga didn't just cum in my ass, and I have to go back in the club. I owed him big time. Since I hadn't cum yet I knew just how to fix him. I finished stroking my dick as he laid up against me. When I was about to cum I turned around and shot off all over his shirt. To make matters worse he was wearing a black shirt and the club was filled with black lights. Now nigga walk around trying to explain what that white shit is on your shirt. If I have to walk around with a drippy ass you have to walk around with my nut on your shirt, I thought.

As soon as I walked back in the club, Michelle started in on me.

"You fucked that nigga you were standing next to at the bar didn't you?"

"Yeah, and!"

We both started laughing and went on dancing to the music. Michelle understands me, and I guess that's why she and I are so close. I don't think I could ever do anything to hurt her. Sometimes I feel like she's the only family that I have.

A few hours later I pulled up to the house where we are going to live. The house was pretty cool. It was a three bedroom, fully furnished house designed for college students. I was unpacking my stuff when a yellow cab pulled up.

"Michelle! Wuz up girl?"

"Eric it's so good to see you. You ready for another bangin' ass year?"

"Hell yeah, I'm looking forward to meeting new ho's to fuck and niggas to suck."

Every now and then I get the urge to fuck a woman. It's not that often, but when I do, I beat the pussy up.

"I feel you on that suckin' nigga part."

"I'm gonna have you eatin' pussy before this year is out, watch!"

"I don't think so."

When I was away from home life was great. I was able to be the bi-sexual I am, without my family bringing me down.

If it was one thing about Michelle I didn't like it was the fact that she is Queen Ghetto. That girl is the kind that bites her toe nails. I walked past her room and saw her putting up empty liquor bottles on her dresser. I just shook my head and walked away. I wanted to tell her, that mini skirt was way too small but that's my girl so I held my tongue. The off campus advisor told me that Michelle and I was going to have to share the house with a student that transferred from another college. He really couldn't tell me much about the person other than they really wanted a house by themselves if they could have accommodated it. That was a bad sign right out the gate. I knew then I wouldn't like who ever was suppose to be moving in. Michelle walked out of her room with that I'm ready to get into something look in her eyes.

"Michelle, before you even open your mouth, we just got here and I'm not trying to go anywhere and get shit started with you."

"Come on Eric, stop trippin'! You know you want to start the year off right so let's go up to the school and tell everybody we see, we're having a small get together."

"Tell everyone we see and a small get together don't go in the same sentence. This is my last year and I need to focus."

"You should have been focused for the last three years. Don't try to make up three years in one semester."

"I have been focused hoochie! That's why this is my last year." She was my girl, but damn she was beginning to work my nerves.

"Look, let's just have a cook out tonight and we don't have

to have another till the spring."

I went along with it just to shut her the hell up. "Fine, Michelle. Fine. But I have a question. Who's paying for the food?"

I knew the answer to that. I knew her broke ass didn't have any money and I was going to have to foot the bill. But that was okay 'cause I'm only buying one slab of ribs and a pound of ground beef for hamburgers. If they asses don't get here while the food is still here, there will be some hungry muthafuckas here tonight.

Later that night the house was packed with almost everybody from the college. There were people outside, in the house, down the street, everywhere. The music was loud and it seemed like everybody that came through the door had either liquor or beer with them. The alcohol was being poured freely. Our party had only been going for about two hours and I was already buzzing. I went outside to get some fresh air. The inside of the house was engulfed with weed smoke. On the patio I met this beautiful woman I had seen a few times on campus last year.

"Hey wuz up? I'm Eric and you are?"

"I'm Danielle"

I tried to act like I wasn't drunk. I had to put my hand on the patio table to steady myself.

"Nice to meet you. I've seen you on campus a few times."

"Yeah, I've noticed you also."

If I didn't know better that sounded like the beginning of her flirting with me. "So, do you have a boyfriend up here or back home?"

"Yeah, he's back home. But I have a saying I live by."

"What's that?"

"Out of sight, out of mind."

That's what I'm talking about. A female that is all about getting hers.

"I tell you what. Let's move this conversation to my room."

She and walked past all the drunk and high people laying on the floor and leaning against the wall.

"You have to excuse my room. I haven't finished unpacking yet. And, I just went to the store and picked up a few things. I keep them in my room to keep people out of it."

She reached in one of the grocery bags that were on the floor.

"I take it you don't like to share your jelly filled doughnuts huh?"

"No, I love my doughnuts. That's why they are in here."

She stood next to the dresser and I sat on the bed. Danielle walked over to me and knelt down between my legs and started tugging on my belt buckle.

"Damn you all about getting yours huh?"

"Shhh! Help me get your pants off."

I stood up and quickly got my pants down around my ankles. Before I could slide my boxers down she was stroking me to the point of erection.

"Eric, I've been wanting to fuck you since last year. You never paid me any attention."

"Well, you damn sure got my attention tonight." I felt her warm mouth lower onto my dick. I laid back and let her do what she wanted to do. She gently nibbled on the head. At first I was shocked but after a while that was an incredible sensation. Besides, I'm all for a little pain.

"You like the way I suck your dick huh?"

I could barely speak. "You good as hell boo."

She went back to doing her thing. She sucked me for what seemed like thirty minuets. I was holding back. I didn't want to cum before she wanted me to. Then she stopped.

"What's wrong? Why you stop?"

"Since you love doughnuts so much." She walked over to the grocery bag on the dresser. Opened up my raspberry filled doughnuts and knelt back between my legs. I didn't know what she was going to do. All I know is I wanted her to put my damn doughnut back.

"What the hell you plan on doing with that. I didn't offer you that doughnut."

She took the doughnut and squished it between her hands. As the jelly ran out she held her hands over my dick as the jelly spilled onto me. My eyes bulged out. She then rubbed her hands all over my dick and thighs. It was doughnut everywhere. She began to suck my dick even harder. All I could hear was the smacking sound of her face hitting the jelly.

"Whoa! Now that's what I'm talking about! Suck the jelly off my dick baby!"

This girl was off the hook. All I could think about was sex with a doughnut, ain't this some shit. I can't wait to try this on somebody else. This is the bomb. The jelly had run all down the crack of my butt and she was right there licking it up.

Right then my bedroom door opened. Danielle and I both looked up. There was this skinny light skinned girl with a very pissed off look on her face, and some dude standing there looking at us. The skinny girl's mouth fell open. She quickly slammed the door. I heard the guy she was with ask her as they walked away from the door, "I hope that was not your roommate."

Damn, I could imagine what she must be thinking. Seeing her new roommate getting his dick sucked with doughnut all over it. I'll go introduce myself after Danielle finishes getting this jelly off of me.

CHAPTER 3

Tracy

"What the hell is going on in this house?" I am so upset it's not funny. My fiancé and I just drove all the way up here from Miami, Florida and the first thing I see when I get here is a house full of drunk ass people and some guy getting his dick sucked.

"Tracy, just calm down. It looks like they're having a welcome back to school party."My fiancé Brandon is always the calm one. I'm about ready to explode.

"Brandon did you see what I just saw? There was a guy lying across a bed with a girl giving him head. I just got here I don't need to be seeing that! This is the reason I wanted a house all to myself. I knew I was going to get stuck with some silly ass people."

As I turned around I looked right into the eyes of the guy that was getting his dick sucked.

"High I'm Eric"

"You nasty. That's what you are!"

"Why it gotta be all that. I came over here to apologize for you seeing that, but if you're gonna trip…"

My teeth clenched as I was about to jump all over this Eric, or what ever he said his name was, person. "Look muthafucka…!"

Brandon jumped in. "Eric, how you doing? My name is Brandon. You have to forgive Tracy. We just drove 13 hours and she's a little grumpy right now."

He had better be glad Brandon jumped in. I was about to read his ass. Eric and Brandon talked for a few more seconds then Eric shot me a nasty look then walked out the room.

"Girl, why are you trippin on your new roommate?"

"My roommate? Oh hell nah!"

"Oh hell yeah. He told me he was your roommate and the other roommate is out there somewhere."

I know all I have to do is pick up the phone and Mama and Daddy will have this fixed first thing in the morning. There was no sense in me even unpacking. Tomorrow I'll be the hell out of here. It's obvious I'm nothing like these people. Daddy works for a major advertising company and mama owns three bakeries. I'm used to the finer things in life. I'm used to people with class. Not these ghetto ass people. I have every right to call the police and have every last one of them picked up for every thing under the sun. Under age drinking. I saw a girl in there, had to be no older than 17 with a beer bottle in her hand. Smoking marijuana, disturbing my peace, everything.

"Tracy, Baby try to calm down. It's not that bad. You partied worse than this when you were at The College of Miami."

I was pacing around the room like an angry beast. Finally after a few more calming words from Brandon I was fine. He even talked me into going out and finding my other roommate and joining the party. Not that I would enjoy talking to anybody in here but at least have a few drinks. I walked towards the bathroom door that was closed. I reached out and turned the knob and the door flew open.

"What the fuck!" I was stunned again.

"Close the door bitch!"

I slammed the door closed and ran back to my room.

"Brandon you are not going to believe what I just saw!"

"What?"

"I opened the door to the bathroom, and there was this big girl bent over the sink getting fucked from the back."

"Really?"

For a second he looked like he wanted to go see for himself. But I guess the snarl on my face prevented that from happening.

"I feel like I just walked into the world's biggest orgy." I just sat on the edge of the bed and put my head in my hands. "This has got to be a bad dream. There is no way I can live with these people."

I looked up and Eric was standing to the door.

"Can I come in?"

"Sure."

He sat down next to me and reintroduced himself to me. Then he started telling me a little bit about himself.

"I'm an elementary education major and I graduate in May. Our roommate Michelle is a little ghetto but she's a good person."

"I haven't met her yet."

"Yes you have, she was the one in the bathroom."

We both looked at each other and busted out laughing. Eric turned out to be okay. Even Brandon was comfortable around him. They seemed to hit it off very well.

It was about 3:00 in the morning and the crowd was dying down. I still hadn't said a word to Michelle. Every time she saw me she looked like she wanted to kick me in the face.

Eric, Brandon, and I sat in my room and talked for hours. Eric told us that he was bi-sexual. I didn't have a problem with it and, surprisingly, neither did Brandon. He seemed almost at ease with it. I'm not the kind of person that gets all into my business with you until I really know you. So, I just told him little things about me. Nothing major.

Since we drove up and I was keeping the car. Brandon had to fly back. His flight left at 7:00 a.m. so he wanted to try and grab a few hours of sleep before he had to go. I wanted to give him some, but by the time Eric left my room, Brandon was snoring and I didn't want to wake him. But something was puzzling me. I could not figure out what that raspberry smell was in my room.

I awoke to the smell of stale beer and marijuana residue. As Brandon lay in the bed, I just laid next to him and tried to soak up the last few minuets he and I had together before he left to go back home. I've been with him for the last eight years. I know everything about him. I know his favorite color, foods, movies, everything. It feels like we were meant to be together. We started dating in the seventh grade. He's been my soul mate since then. We have plans on getting married and starting our own Gourmet Bakery one day. Since he's majoring in Business Administration and I'm in my junior year majoring in Culinary Arts it just seems obvious the career path we have chosen.

As he awoke and started to stretch, the early morning sun peaking through the blinds hit his body at the perfect angle. He is my Adonis. All six foot four inches of him belongs to me. His dark skin seems to glisten as the sun reflects of his well toned chest. I rolled over ready to offer him my body before he left.

"Oh shit baby. My plane leaves in forty five minuets!"

My bubble was burst just that fast.

After seeing Brandon off at the airport, I went back to the house to try to get things situated. I really do like Eric, but I'm still not sure if I was going to stay or not. When I walked in Eric was in the kitchen on the phone. Michelle was sitting on the couch watching T.V. I walked in and introduced myself.

She said, "What's up?" Without even looking at me.

I sat down beside her and started asking her questions about herself. "Where are you from?"

"Orlando."

"Great, I'm from Miami. What's your major?"

"P.E."

"How old are you?"

"20."

Michelle was acting like I was irritating her. I guess Eric got the same impression, because he came in the room and started asking me questions about Miami. I told him about South Beach, Aventura Mall, Bayside, and many of the popular tourist attractions. He told me he always wanted to go there because it sounded so exotic. Miami has its moments. I never really got to enjoy most of it, because my parents are so strict. They never wanted me to venture into Liberty City, Overtown, Opa-Locka, or any of the predominantly black neighborhoods. Most people can't believe I was born and raised in Miami and have never been to any of the many clubs that line South Beach. If my parents had caught me even thinking about going, they would have killed me. Since Brandon is a P.K., we spend most of our time in church or youth conferences. My parents loved him from the first time they met him and found out he was Bishop Billy Robbins' son. He's the pastor of one of the newest black churches in Miami. To my mother and father Brandon's family was on the rise and the two families got along, they just figured that Brandon and I should be together forever. They think he is so perfect. Little do they know, he is the one that taught me all I know about sex and pleasing a man.

Eric and I walked outside to unpack more stuff out of my car. "Eric, what's the deal with your girl Michelle? I tried to start a conversation with her and she gave me all these one word answers."

"Well, that's Michelle, straight out the ghetto. She'll get better once you get to know her."

"Acting like that, I don't know if I want to get to know her, she ain't gotta worry. I won't say shit else to her."

"Come on now, why it got to be like that? Can't we all just get along?"

"Huh, yeah we'll see. Anyway, what's up with you being bisexual? The way that girl was all up on that the other night shows me you love the ladies."

"Oh no my sister, I LOVE me some men. I just have to have my taste of a woman every now and then. If I had to choose one, I'll take a nice long dick any day. Besides it has a lot to do with my uncle when I was growing up."

Right then I knew exactly what he was talking about so I just shut my mouth and kept unpacking. Eric helped me take the last two boxes in the house to my room. "So, Tracy, what made you transfer all the way to North Carolina?"

"Well, the main reason is I had to get away from a situation that was just getting way out of control. The reason I told my parents is because Bell University has the best culinary arts program in the country. It helps too that my mother is an alumni. So of course she didn't protest."

"Tracy, I can't even start to think that a girl like you would get caught up in something that would make you leave the state."

"Eric, we all have our skeletons."

While I was talking to Eric my cell phone rang. I looked at the caller ID and damn near dropped the phone. Sometimes skeletons come out the closet and get packed with your luggage.

CHAPTER 4

Michelle

No that bitch didn't just try to start a conversation with me. The first words out of her mouth to me should have been I'm sorry for walking in the bathroom on you last night. Then I might have a few words for her. But, I see already she thinks she's too big to apologize. I'll fix her ass, you best believe that.

I'm sitting on the sofa watching T.V. when Eric walks out of Tracy's room. "So, I see you have a new best friend."

"Don't start. She just wanted me to help her get the rest of her things out her car."

Walking over to the front room window I asked Eric, "What kind of car does she drive?"

"It's the new SVT Cobra Mustang. It's off the hook too!"

"Whatever." I should have known she was one of those rich kids whose parents buy them everything. Don't have to work for shit. Just say Daddy I need, and it's there for you. I feel like if I stay in this house another second, and Miss Thang walk in here, I'm going to kick her ass.

"Eric, let's go up to campus since classes start tomorrow. This might be a good time to hit the book store." Upper classmen always got our class syllabus early to make sure we were able to show up to class day one ready to work.

"Yeah, sounds good. Let me ask Tracy if she wants to go."

"Let's leave her ass here. She's all locked up in her room, no need to disturb her."

"Even though I know you're trippin', I'll go along with you this time."

As we walked down the drive way I looked at Tracy's car.

Eric was right, it was hot. Hot pink custom paint job. Black leather interior. Bose speakers. This car was loaded. I took my key and ran it down the side of that perfect little Barbie car as I walked by it. Eric was walking in front of me, so he didn't see what I was doing. We got in his car and he looked over at me.

"What the hell are you smiling so wide about?"

"Nothing, I'm just happy that's all"

On the way to campus Eric started a conversation I really didn't feel like having.

"So. How's your mom doing?"

"She's fine I guess."

"Have you called her and told her you made it here okay?"

"No. I'll call her later this week. Now can we change the topic?" I hate talking about my mother. It always brings up very bad memories for me. I try not to call her too often. Maybe once a month. And I make sure it's during the middle of the week when I know she's not home. We turned onto the campus and my spirits jumped up. I couldn't hold my tongue as we rode around.

"Look at all these fine ass niggas! It's like a buffet of USDA Grade A dick around here."

"I know girl. Since this is my last year I'm on a mission to fuck one person."

"Who?"

"Thomas Clark."

"He's the president of Phi Kappa Gamma. The most popular fraternity on campus. And, if you hadn't realized it. He's not gay."

"No, he's not gay. But he is bi."

"How do you know?"

"All I'm going to say is that we are from the same small town of Danville, Va. There are no secrets there."

Shaking my head, I turned and kept looking at the fine men walking around our beautiful campus. Over the last two years I've developed a reputation of a wild party girl. Some of that is true I will try anything once. I have taken my share of other women's boyfriends at parties and had sex with them in bathrooms, outside, in the car, wherever I want to do it at. So, that makes me a well-hated woman on campus. It's not my fault their men want this. Speaking of men wanting this, there is Craig Johnson. He's the star linebacker for our football team. He's dating some little skinny girl with bad hair. She thinks she's all that, but we'll see how she feels when I fuck her man this year.

"Eric, let me out the car I have to holla at Craig right quick."

"You want me to wait on you?"

"Nah, meet me at the library in an hour all right."

"An hour Michelle. Don't have me leave your ass."

I pulled my skirt up a little as I got out the car. I wanted to show off these thick thighs guys go crazy over. My halter-top showed off these double D's. I had on my calf strap heels and I know that I am going to turn heads today. I looked Craig right in his eyes as I walked up to him. The lust was in his eyes was evident. He wanted me and he wanted me bad.

"Craig, how have you bee?. How was your summer?"

"I'm good. Took the summer to bulk up a little. You look like you worked out a little."

His deep voice was melting my heart. I wanted to climb on top of him right where he stood. My eyes roamed up and down his body. He constantly looked around making sure his little girlfriend didn't walk up on us talking.

"I'm not gonna beat around the bush. You know I've been trying to get with you for the last two years. What's the problem?"

"The problem is I have a girlfriend."

"So, I'm not trying to be your wife, I just want to get broke off every now and then." I'm very straight forward and to the point about things I want. He's the typical guy. I put the pressure on him and he don't want the reputation of being scared of the pussy so I know I'll be getting some of him real soon.

"I tell you what. Come to my room around 11:30 tonight. My girl will be back at her place by then. We'll get up then."

I gave him a sexy smile and kissed him on the cheek. He gave me his room and phone number. "11:30 tonight," he repeated before I walked off.

As I walked around the campus trying to kill an hour, I

noticed several guys looking and staring at me. This was the perfect time for me to find my money source for the year. I walked over to the freshmen male dorm. I knew the resident advisor so I walked in to talk to him for a while. Actually I needed a reason to go inside the dorm. Freshmen boys are the horniest, most gullible things on the planet. Show them a piece of the titty and they are in love, giving you all the little money they parents are sending them. I walked into the dorm and it went silent. All the guys were standing around mouths open. The resident advisor walked out and saw me and turned and started laughing. He knew what I was doing so he let me do my thing. The resident advisor was a friend of mine. We started school here together. We've fucked a couple of times but we always kept it as just that. A fuck. Being the advisor of the dorm paid for his room and board and gave him a little money in his pocket.

I looked for the guy that looked like he had the most money. All the so called big money boys tried to grab my attention. I talked to a few of them but I was looking for something else. I found my money bag sitting in front of the T.V. with his Dell Laptop computer. He wasn't wearing a lot of jewelry or a throw back jersey. He was just an average looking guy that I could just tell parents was hooking him up.

"Hey cutie, what's up?" He looked up and glanced around the room to see if I was really talking to him. He was actually very cute. He was wearing a navy Tommy Hilfiger polo, a pair of khakis and some white Reebok Classics. The nigga smelled good too. He's not the type of guy I would typically kick it with. I had a different agenda, so it didn't matter much anyway.

"Uh, uh nothing, how are you?" He stared at me like he was in a daze.

"I'm good, better now that I have seen you. By the way, my name is Michelle."

"I'm Prentice. Prentice Ellis. It's very nice to meet you."

His name even sounds like he has money. I could tell he wasn't use to getting much play from the women. He acted very shy. This was going to be easier than I thought. "Are you a freshman?"

"Yeah, I'm a chemical engineer major. What about you?"

"I'm a junior, P.E major, nothing exciting. I really want to get to know you more. Would you like to walk me over to the library so we can just talk alone for a second?"

"Sure." He packed his computer in his bag and stood up to walk me to the door. I could see him eyeing my butt as I walked by him. I put a little more jiggle in it 'cause I knew he was watching. I waited for him while he put his computer in the trunk of a cute little black Honda Accord.

"I can drive you to the library?"

"No I want to walk so we can spend a little time together"

This muthafucka is way too easy. Prentice told me he was from Columbus, Ohio. His father was a pediatric dentist and his mother was into real estate. He had one older brother that was a movie producer, and two younger sisters. He likes to play golf, read poetry, and cook. He didn't have a girlfriend. He didn't date much in high school. I forgot all the other stuff he told me because I really didn't care. I just wanted to make sure he had some money. We exchanged numbers, and I told him I would give him a call sometime so we could hang out. He smiled from ear to ear. I left him standing there looking like the Cheshire Cat.

Eric was waiting for me when I got inside. "It's about time your hoochie ass got here."

"Don't hate player. What did you get into? Did you see your boy, Thomas?"

"Yeah, I saw him, but he was with his line brothers. Believe me, I will have my turn alone with him. I can just taste him now."

"We will see nigga. I don't think you have a chance in hell."

"Now who's hating?"

"Eric let's go, I got to go home and freshen this coochie up for tonight."

"Who you fucking now? I hope it's not that fine little boy you was just talking to."

"Naw nigga, that's just how I'm going to keep my pockets full. I'm finally going to give that Craig something to talk about. So, can you be a dear and drop me off on campus tonight?"

"Girl, you need to get your own car and leave me out of your hoe-hopping."

"I'll be ready by 11:15."

"I'm not picking your ass up either."

"Don't worry, I'll have a ride home."

Tracy wasn't home when we got there. I was glad to see her prissy ass gone. I went to my room to get out my gear for tonight. I didn't want to get too dressed up. It was going to all end up on the floor anyway. I picked out a black sheer tank top and a pair of low cut jeans. My new black lace bra and thong set would look great under that. It was only 9:00, so I had a little time before I had to be over at Craig's. I turned on the radio. Big Poppa by Biggie Smalls was playing. I love that song, but it made me remember that night about five years ago. Mama had lost some more money that she didn't have.

"Michelle, Big Willie needs to come back and talk to you."

Big Willie came in my room; I already knew what the deal was so I got down on my knees. I had been paying my mother's debts for about two years at that point. Big Willie told me to get up. He wanted something different tonight. He wanted to fuck my ass. I told that nigga he was crazy. All I could think about was the pain that would cause. He begged and pleaded for me to give it to him. He finally told me he would give me fifty dollars if I let him stick it in. Money. That was a different story. My mother taught me to do damn near anything for money.

I took his money and slipped my pants off. He grabbed my Vaseline off my dresser and coated his dick with it. They sure as hell didn't call him Big Willie because of his dick size. It couldn't have been any wider than my thumb. I tried to relax as he bent me over and started to push through my virgin hole. I guess since he was so small it didn't hurt as bad as I anticipated. He pumped about a good three times then yelled like he was having a baby. Next thing I knew nut was running down my butt cheeks. He pulled his pants up and walked out. Damn, that was the quickest and easiest fifty dollars I ever made. That night I learned two things. One, I was starting to like the benefits of sex and two, how easy men part with their money.

Eric dropped me off at Miller Hall. That was the athlete's dorm. It was made coed last year. I walked in, and of course the niggas was staring like dogs in heat. I walked up the stairs to room 262 and knocked on the door. Craig answered wearing nothing but some gym shorts. I was about to jump on his ass right there, but I noticed his teammate Jason sitting on the bed. Craig let me in and closed the door behind me. "I hope you don't mind the company?"

Craig knew I was coming over to fuck, so I guess he told his boy to come get some too. "No, I don't mind. I can handle both of you." I didn't care if I had to do the whole football team, as long as I got a piece of Craig. "Anyway, the more the merrier."

I walked over to the door and hit the light switch. I almost jumped out my skin, when the room came to life with little stickers they had put all over the wall that glowed, when Craig's silly butt turned a black light on. I guess they thought that was sexy or something but it didn't matter to me. I was there to get mine. Both guys sat on the bed as I turned on the radio to 98.6, the slow jam station. The music was hot. I started to slowly dance in front of both of them. My ass wiggled to the beat of the music. I looked and saw that both Jason and Craig were getting harder and harder. Jason stood up and took off his pants. He had a thick dick but I was interested in Craig's thickness.

I got down on my knees, closed my eyes and opened my mouth. What ever went in, I was sucking. I felt the smooth skin of a hard dick past my lips. I opened my eyes and it was Craig sliding his monster size dick into my face. I wanted to give him the best head he had ever gotten. I was so into Craig that I didn't notice Jason laying on the floor behind me. I felt him lift my butt cheeks and slide under me. I was sitting on Jason's dick with his boy's dick in my mouth. I tried to break his damn pelvis; I fucked him so hard. I let Craig's dick fall from my mouth.

"Which one of you are gonna cum for me first?" I must admit Jason's dick was good as I bounced my ass up and down on him. Every so often he would smack me on the ass. That was a turn on for me. I loved when a guy smacked me on the butt or pulled my hair. Craig walked over and put his dick back in my mouth. Bouncing on a dick while sucking one is a dream come true to a freak like me. I had two big hard dicks to do what ever I pleased with. I was in paradise. After a few minuets I got up off Jason. "Craig, come fuck me from the back."

Jason turned the music up because all of us were starting to get a little loud. I bent over the bed and let Craig jam his dick into me. Finally I had his ass. I clinched my pussy muscles to tighten myself up a little. I wanted him to come back for more after tonight. I was lost in lust.

"Talk dirty to me Craig. Call me names. Tell me that I'm a slut!"

That must have gotten them both turned on.

"Take this dick, dirty bitch!"

"Yeah baby that's it. Give mama all that big dick!"

Jason jumped in "Shut the fuck up and suck my dick!" He walked over and slapped me in the face with his dick then shoved it in my mouth. I could feel my heart start to pick up pace. Craig was ramming me hard. It was like he was reading my mind. He grabbed my hair and pulled back on it. I let Jason's dick fall out of my mouth for a brief second.

"That's what I'm talking about. Pull my hair daddy!"

It was like I had a sixth sense about when a guy was about to cum. I could tell before they could. Jason's dick got extremely hard in my mouth I knew it was only a matter of seconds before he came.

"I want you to drink my cum bitch!"

As soon as he was ready to cum I pulled off his dick and let him cum all over the floor.

"Damn girl! I wanted to cum in your mouth!"

"I'm not your girlfriend nigga."

Craig was still going strong. His thrusts were getting stronger by the second. I had cum about three times all over his dick. The smacking sound of his dick hitting my pussy was making us both uncontrollable. He grabbed two handfuls of my ass. I knew he was getting close. I started throwing my ass back at him as he fucked me. I could feel the pulse in his dick.

"Shoot it on my ass baby!"

"Here it comes…aghh!" I felt warm cum fall all over my butt. I jiggled my ass as he stroked the last few drops from his dick. I laid flat on my stomach across the bed. Both Jason and Craig were tired as hell. I got up and walked over and turned on the lights. Of course Jason started talking first.

"What's up Boo? We ain't done."

"Yes you are," I said with a stern voice.

"Craig, tell your girl to get over here and suck my dick!"

Before Craig could say a word I was all over him. "First of all I didn't want to fuck you in the first place I wanted to fuck your boy, but since you were here I just gave you some mercy pussy! Secondly, I told you before; I'm not your girl. You demand shit from her! The only reason I let you talk to me like that before was because I was caught up in the moment but rest assured that won't happen again!"

Craig didn't open his mouth. And neither did Jason for that matter. I got dressed and headed for the door.

"Craig, you were wonderful. I hope we can do this again real soon. Just next time, leave Curious George home okay."

Jason do kinda look like a monkey the more I think about it. I winked at Craig and walked out the room closing the door behind me. I walked over to the freshman dorm to look for my friend Prentice so he could take me home.

CHAPTER 5

Eric

While Michelle was out doing her thing, Tracy and I sat on the sofa and watched B.E.T. It was late and both of us had taken our baths and was ready for bed. I had on my favorite red and black flannel pants with a wife beater. She was wearing a pair of Joe Boxers and an old Roca Wear tee shirt. I was all into the videos, when she just started talking.

"Have you ever done something in your life that you regret? And, no matter how hard you try to put it behind you, it just keeps coming up?"

I sat there for a second and thought about my answer. From the look on her face something was eating away at her. "Yes. Once I stole some money out of my mom's purse and got caught. From then on she's always held her purse close to her whenever I came around."

Tracy just looked at me and laughed a little. I knew that's not exactly what she was talking about. But I didn't want to make her situation about me 'cause I have a tendency to listen to another person's problems and end up telling all my business.

"Eric, if I tell you something you promise not to tell another soul?"

Damn, this was getting deep. She must have killed somebody and was under an alias trying to run from the police. Okay. My imagination got the best of me for a second.

"Yes, I promise."

She took a deep breath. She looked at me with tears in her eyes. I could see that whatever she was about to tell me was hurting her. All the wild things I imagined she was going to say left me. I was really concerned about her. Placing my hand over hers I said, "Whatever is on your mind, you can talk to me about it."

"Okay. Last year down in Miami, I..."

Ring...Ring...Ring. My cell phone started ringing. "Hold up just one second." I dropped her hand and went into my room to grab my phone. "Hello?"

"Eric, you are not gonna believe the fun I had tonight!"

"Michelle, is this you?"

"Yeah. I fucked Craig and his roommate Jason at the same time."

"No you didn't! Was it good?"

"Hell yeah! Both of them have big thick dicks."

"Damn girl, tell me everything. I want to know everything about them, inch by inch."

"Well, I'll tell you about it when I get home. I'm on my way to the freshmen boy's dorm to get my new friend to bring me home."

I sat on the edge of my bed for another five minuets giddy as a little girl at her first sleep over. "Oh shit. I forgot all about Tracy." I said to myself, as I jumped up and went back into the front room. Tracy was knocked out sleep. Evidently she was sleeping hard 'cause her mouth was open and she was snoring loud enough to wake the dead. I walked into her room and grabbed her comforter off the bed. Placing it over her, she smiled a little. Whatever she was dreaming about was making her happy. That's a big difference from the tear soaked eyes I had just seen. I'm sure whatever was on her mind, she'd get around to telling me another day. I walked back into her room, because I noticed a picture of Brandon on her dresser.

Whispering to myself I said, "Damn that's a fine ass nigga." Picking up the picture I knew that there was something different about him. I had to find out more. I went to the door and listened to see if Tracy was still snoring. After a few seconds I realized that she was louder now than she was before. In Tracy's room was something like a make shift shrine set up of him. Pictures of him in swim trunks. Pictures of him dressed up. The most gorgeous one was the picture of him standing on the beach without his shirt on, with the sun setting behind him. Looking around the room I noticed a note pad on the night stand next to the bed. The note pad had a picture of an angel on it. I picked it up and turned to the first page.

2/14/03

Dear journal,

I don't know what to do. Brandon wants to take me out tonight. But he has demanded that I go out with him. My heart belongs to Brandon. I've put myself in this situation. I have nobody to blame but me. I can't believe that I'm still going through with this. I told myself never again. But every time I see him, I just have to. I need to get myself together. Brandon is whom I desperately desire. He was a mistake. I've said that to myself over and over again but I still keep going back. Today I found out that now I'm a willing participant.

"Damn, my girl had a little situation down there in Miami," I said to myself. I turned the page. Suddenly headlights ran across the room. I closed the note pad and put it back on the nightstand. Running out of Tracy's room I kicked over a glass of water. "Oh, shit."

I looked for something to clean it up with. I heard a car door close outside. In a few seconds Michelle's keys would be in the door and that was sure to wake Tracy up. I looked around frantically and found a pair of cotton panties lying on the bed. I threw the panties over the spill. I used the extra cotton crotch part to try and soak up the water. I figured if they could contain her wetness, they should contain this one. The front door opened and sure enough I heard Tracy yawn. I balled the underwear up and shoved them in my pocket. The bathroom was right next to Tracy's room so I acted like I was coming out of there.

"You finally made it home huh?"

Michelle turned and had the biggest smile on her face. "Wait till I tell you about my night!"

Tracy stood up and wrapped herself in the comforter. "I'm going to bed. See ya'll in the morning."

As she walked away, Michelle started. "Shit, I didn't want to talk about it in front of her anyway."

"Why do you hate on her so much?"

Michelle frowned. It was like she had smelled rotten eggs and fish at the same time.

"I hate people like her."

"What do you mean, people like her"

Sucking her teeth she said, "Do you want to know about my night or what!"

"Yeah heffa, tell me."

Michelle went on to tell me about her escapades with Craig and Jason. I swear that girl is a true freak. She reminds me of a female version of me. I can just imagine all the freaky things I'm going to do to Thomas when I get my hands on him.

I must have died and gone to Heaven. I walked in my reading and diagnosis class, and the man of my dreams was sitting there flashing that killer smile at the ladies. These gold digging hoochies don't have nothing on me. Thomas is every bit of 6'2 195 pounds. He has a milk chocolate complexion and eyes that melt your heart. I made my way over and sat in the seat to his left. I wanted to speak but Professor Long walked in and started class. Reading and diagnosis is a senior class that teaches how to identify factors and study the various causes of reading disabilities. Professor Long explained to us what our group project was to be this semester. I heard the word group and my eyes lit up. I was going to make sure I ended up in Thomas's group. That would help me make my move.

The project seems pretty simple. We have to asses the reading abilities of a group of school children and implement the appropriate courses of treatment. We had to form groups of four.

"Thomas, man what's up? How was your summer?" I asked finally getting to look into his big brown eyes.

"Man it was good. Too short; I spent most of the summer doing an internship at Miles Elementary."

"Cool. Why don't we work together this year on the project?" Hoping he would say yes.

"Not a problem, all we need are two more willing participants, and we can start working on our A."

Right on cue, the two skanks he was talking to earlier sashayed their way over to join our little duo. Don't get me wrong, Skye and Misa are beautiful females, but I don't need them cock blocking. They both want Thomas just as much as I do. I can tell by the way they throw that fake laugh every time he opens his mouth.

We all agreed to meet in the student union at 4:00 to go over the plans for the project. It's 3:40 when I get there. I sit down just in time to see Thomas strutting up the steps. He sees me, and give me some dap.

"Eric, this is going to be one helluva year. We have two beautiful ladies to work with. Skye is fine, but Misa, she has those beautiful Asian eyes, and ghetto booty. You should try to hook up with Skye. I plan to bend Misa over first chance I get."

If I don't bend yours over first. I thought. "I can't disagree with you on that. Skye is a dime piece, but I got my eye on another treasure I want to dig into." I said while licking my lips. Thomas looked at me with curious eyes but didn't comment. I'm sure he knows about my sexuality, and I don't plan to hide the fact I want him for a five-course meal.

CHAPTER 6

Tracy

As I drove to class this morning my cell phone rang. I looked at the caller I.D. and a cold feeling came over me. I knew who it was. In the nastiest voice I could muster I said, "Hello!"

"Why do you have to sound so mean , so early in the morning?"

"Why are you calling me!"

"Because I miss you."

"Look, I told you before to stop calling me. I've moved and soon I'll have another phone and you'll never be able to call me again!"

"I wouldn't be so sure of that"

The phone went silent. After a few seconds I heard the dial tone. I tossed my phone in the passenger seat. I thought, why ruin my first day of class.

I pulled into the parking lot and walked into the building where my class was being held. I heard several professors already teaching and lecturing. I walked down the hall looking for room number thirty four. The closer I got to the room I heard a very familiar voice. I thought, *I know that voice.* But there is no chance in hell…

I walked into the class and there he stood. Professor Caldwell. I wanted to turn and run from the class. But I was not going to give him the luxury of seeing me run out of his class. He looked at me and a slight grin ran across his face. "Good morning."

I wanted to curse him on the spot. However, being the woman I am, I just nodded my head and found a seat way in the back of the class. For the entire hour I felt like Professor Caldwell was staring at me. His eyes almost pierced through me. I hated the way he looked through a person. I noticed all the other women in the class were hanging on his every word. I even overheard one of the girls in the class tell her friend, "I'll never miss this class. That muthafucka is too fine."

I rolled my eyes. He wasn't all that. Yeah he's tall, light skinned, and has a body that looks like he was cut from stone. But, he had nothing on my Brandon.

At the end of class I just wanted to walk out without him saying a word to me. But my luck just wasn't that good.

"Tracy, can I talk to you for a second?"

I stopped dead in my tracks. I flung my head around in his direction "What? What do you possibly have to say to me?"

I had forgotten that there were still a few other students in the class. They looked at me as if I had lost my mind talking to a professor like that.

"I just wanted to say, I hope we have a great year. And that I hope we can let our past stay there."

I didn't say a word. I just walked away. He must think I'm some silly freshman. I saw right through that shit. He didn't say what he really wanted to say because there were still a few stragglers left in the classroom. I walked as fast as I could to the Drop and Add department. That's where you go if you want to drop a class or add a class to your schedule. I walked over to the counter and grabbed a form to get out of his class. I handed it to the lady behind the counter.

"I'm sorry. This is the only time that class is being offered this year."

"Are you serious?" I wanted to pass out. I was stuck in that man's class. Food and Nutrition is a required course I have to take this year in order to graduate on time. For the rest of the day I was a complete wreck. I was angry at the world. I snapped at people for no reason. I was a pissed off sister. After my last class I decided to just go home and call Brandon. He always knew what to say to make me feel better.

I stepped out my car in front of the house and the smell of pan grease and fish was in the air. I wanted to throw up. "Whoever is cooking that shit needs to die. That smells awful." I noticed the closer to the front door I got, the stronger the smell got. Opening the door I was rushed by that awful stench that was coming from the kitchen. Michelle decided to cook fish and grits in the middle of the day. I stood to the door and she just looked at me and turned her head and kept cooking. I knew that nasty smell was going to be in the furniture and all over everything. I just hope it was not in any of my clothes. A few minuets later I heard Eric walked in the house.

"What the fuck is that smell. Smells like a dead cat up in here."

"Don't hate. You know this shit smell good." Michelle's ghetto ass couldn't tell you what good food smelled like. All she knows is greens, fried chicken, fried fish, fried cornbread, fried okra, and anything else fried. I see why her ass is so big. Eric knocked on my door.

"Come in."

He walked in and lay across my bed. "So, how was your day?"

"It was okay. I just have to deal with a teacher I don't like."

"Which one? I know them all."

"Professor Caldwell. He teaches my Food and Nutrition class."

"You don't mean that new fine ass nigga with the funny color eyes do you? Hell girl, I'll take your place in his class any day. All you little bitches running around talking about him."

I know he was making a little joke but the situation was not funny to me at all. "Byron and I...I mean Professor Caldwell and I don't get along too well."

"Byron? Damn, you know him like that already?"

"Well it's like this...." Just as I was about to tell Eric why he and I don't get along, there was another knock at my door.

"Eric come out here and eat some of this fish."

"Wait a minuet okay?"

"No! Come on. Ain't nothing worse than cold, soggy fried fish." I looked at Eric with a very irritated look on my face.

"Tracy don't let her get to you. She's just mad I don't want none of her soggy fish. If you know what I mean."

"Damn man it's just every time you're in here she always finds a reason to call you away. I think she hates it when we talk."

"You have to understand. She and I have been through a lot together over the years and she can get a little jealous."

Eric walked out the room. I leaned over and grabbed my phone off the dresser to call Brandon. Brandon is my rock. He's my soul mate. He took me back after I had hurt him in the worst possible way. I know in my heart that he is the one for me.

When his cell started ringing I instantly was overcome with excitement. He was the only man that ever made me feel this way.

When his phone picked up I was just about to start the conversation with I love you, when a voice I didn't recognize spoke to me.

"Hello?" I sat there for a second trying to catch the voice. "Hello is anybody there?"

"I'm sorry I must have dialed the wrong number." I hung up the phone and sat on the edge of the bed knowing I had dialed the correct number. This time I carefully watched my finger press every number on the dial pad.

"Hello?"

"Brandon?"

"Yeah."

"Hey boo, the funniest thing just happened. I could have sworn I dialed your number and somebody else answered the phone."

"My phone didn't ring at all"

"Okay, then I must have messed up. So, how has your day been?"

"It's been great, but I'm a little busy right now. Can I call you back later?"

Normally, Brandon will stop whatever he is doing to talk to me, but something wasn't right, and I really didn't feel like getting into it with him.

"Yeah that's fine. Call me sometime tonight I'll be home."

"Aiight then."

I started to call back again in a few minuets but I figured

that would just get him to start thinking I was up to something and I don't need that right now.

I decided to go for a little run around the neighborhood. I put on my gray running body suit and sneakers and headed for the door. I walked past Michelle and Eric sitting at the kitchen table eating that funky ass fish. Eric looked up at me

"Where you going looking like Flo Jo?"

"I like to run when I have things on my mind."

Just then Michelle raised her grease stained face from her plate. "Well if you gonna run, run. Stop talking 'bout it and go."

I wanted to snatch that plate from under her three chins and smack the hell out of her with it.

"Instead of sitting there looking like a bear eating fish, you should come run with me. On second thought, never mind. I don't have time to do CPR on you when you pass out after two steps."

She jumped up from the table like she was gonna come after me. But Eric grabbed her arm and made her sit back down. Before she could say another word I was out the door. I heard her mumbling something as the door closed behind me. It felt good to tell that fat bitch off. I never liked her ever since I walked in on her fucking in the bathroom that night. As I walked past my car I noticed a long deep scratch on the passenger side of my car.

"What the fuck!" I knew that damn Michelle had something to do with it. But, I couldn't prove it, so I just let it go.

Running was always a way I could clear my mind. And, at this point my mind needed clearing: the phone situation with Brandon, and now Byron. I don't know whether to keep running all the way to Miami or just go to my room and stay there for the rest of the year. Before I realized it, I had run at least two miles away from the house. I wasn't too far from the college campus. I decided to run around the campus. It would be a good way for me to see everything. The school is beautiful. There are flowers that line each driveway. And huge Magnolia trees all over the campus. We also have several statues of famous black scholars and humanitarians.

I was startled by the sound of a car honking its horn and coming in my direction. As the car got closer I realized who it was behind the wheel. The car pulled along side of me. I tried to act like I didn't see or hear it. The car window rolled down as Byron was trying to get my attention.

"Tracy we need to talk."

"Does it have anything to do with class?"

"No."

"Then we have nothing to talk about."

"Yes we do. Stop trippin' and get in."

"Hell no, I'm not getting into your car. As a matter of fact, I need to file a complaint against you for sexual harassment. Asking me to get in your car as I'm jogging down the street wearing my body suit. See the little twist I can put on it."

"Yeah I see. But when it comes out that you and I have a past, and that you followed me up here from Miami. All that kinda wrecks your poor little case. Do you think they will believe some snot nose stuck up little girl, or an award winning professor with high recommendations from every top college professor in the south east."

"I followed you up here? Nigga please!"

"See, you're not the only one with a little twist. Now get the fuck in the car!"

I stood there for a second. I thought: He's right. If I went to anybody about it, he would just deny it and I would end up looking like the little college girl with a crush on her teacher.

I walked around to the passenger side and got in. "Where are we going?"

"To my house."

"For what?"

"To make up for lost time."

I wanted to jump out the car every time we stopped at a light. I sat in the car getting sicker and sicker by the second 'cause I knew what he wanted. I prayed that something happened to the car and we couldn't make it to his place. Just then, the gas bell rang and the gaslight came on.

"Damn I have to get gas!"

We pulled into a BP gas station.

I said under my breath, "Please go in and pay for the gas." I waited for him to walk toward the building so I could jump out. He got out the car and reached for his wallet.

"Damn that muthafuckas gonna use his debit card."

Sure enough he got out and stood in front of the pumps and swiped his card. I was in a situation I didn't want to be in at that moment. He was keeping a very close eye on me to make sure I didn't do anything sudden.

I looked around and saw Eric pulling into the pumps next to us. I jumped out the car.

"Eric, wuz up man?"

I looked back and Byron had a horrible look on his face. Eric didn't know it but he had just saved me from being with Byron.

"Tracy, oh I'm sorry. Hello Professor Caldwell."

"Hey how are you doing?"

"I'm good sir."

This was my chance to get away. "Well thank you Professor Caldwell for the ride. This is my roommate; he'll take me the rest of the way." I got in Eric's car and closed the door.

"Okay Tracy. I'll see you in class."

I could tell he was mad enough to spit fire but there was nothing he could do. He was not gonna make a scene. So he just let me go. After Eric pumped the gas he got in the car.

"Where were y'all going?"

"Back to his place"

"For real? Damn girl, you fuckin' a teacher?"

"No I'm not fuckin him, but there is something I need to tell you about him."

Just then that old Earth Wind and Fire song "In the Stone" came on the radio.

"Oh that's my jam!" Eric turned the radio up as loud as he could get it. Another blown opportunity for me to tell him what was really going on.

CHAPTER 7

Michelle

How dare that bitch call me a bear? I should knock her ass out on the spot for that shit. But me being the lady that I am, is just gonna walk away from beating her ass. But one thing I do know is that something is going on with her. I don't know what it is, but she always wants Eric to talk to her in private about something. Since Eric and Tracy are both gone, I might as well do a little looking around that hoe's room to find out what's the deal. I walked into her room and started going through her dresser drawers looking for anything that might tip me off. I quickly found out that Tracy is one boring bitch. I couldn't find a thing that I could use to make that bitch miserable.

I've never liked people that thought they were better than me. I hate those light skin, long fake hair, press on nails bitches. They think just because they look a certain way that they are better than me or that their pussy is better than mine. From what I hear those bitches are the worst ones in bed. Just lay there looking good but the sex is horrible. My sister is one of those light skin women and Mama never made her sleep with any of them stankin' ass niggas from the neighborhood. It was always me 'cause my butt was bigger, and I had bigger lips. My sister was petite, thin lips, narrow hips. And Mama always tried to tell us we had the same daddy. There was no way in hell we had the same dad. I saw him before. That nigga was tall and black as night. Mama ain't no red bone herself. So where did this snow bunny come from? Mama always made her to be better than me for some reason. I was the child she called when it was time to pay off her dept. My sister was the child she called when she wanted to show off her kids.

I walked over to her night stand. In the top drawer was a note pad with an angel on the cover. I opened it and realized it was Tracy's journal. I flipped through a few pages and finally came across something I felt I could use.

3/18/03

Today was beautiful. Byron and I made love for hours today. I can barely walk. I know that if Brandon finds out what I'm doing behind his back he'll be devastated. But I have to live for me. Sometimes I want to break it off with Byron because I feel if it gets out that he is sleeping with one of his students then it will hurt both of us. I don't know what I would do if that happened. My family has pretty much groomed me to be Brandon's wife. He's even been on family vacations with my family. I love Brandon and don't want to hurt him but I have to be true to my heart. Byron makes me happy. I never thought I could feel this way about any man that wasn't Brandon. I am truly in a love triangle.

"That dirty bitch!" She was cheating on her man. Miss Prissy ain't so fuckin' innocent. I fumbled through a few more pages I was trying to find this Byron person's last name. I figured if I can find it where they first met she might have put his last name in the book. As I looked for his name I read about the time she and Byron did it in his office. She even talked about sitting in the front row of his class with no underwear on. She wrote: Every time he walked by I would spread my legs so he could see what he would be getting later.

"That bitch was fucking a teacher." Finally, almost in the front of the book I found what I was looking for:

12/15/02

I don't know what came over me today. Mr. Caldwell was in the middle of teaching and I just winked at him and licked my lips. After I did it I just sat there hoping that he didn't see it. After class he called me to his desk. I walked in and he offered me a soda. I told him I was sorry for my behavior and he said that he had noticed me from the first day of class and always wanted to say something to me. He walked over to me and leaned in to kiss me. What was really shocking was that I didn't resist. We kissed like old lovers. His large hands roamed all over my body. I pulled away and we just stared at each other. He told me to call him Byron and we exchanged numbers. I don't know what I've started but I think I just assured myself an A in his class.

"Byron Caldwell. For some reason that name sounds familiar to me." I put the journal back in the drawer and walked out of her room. I was sure I had heard that name somewhere before. I have an aunt that works down at the College of Miami. I asked her about Byron Caldwell. From what she told me, he transferred to a school here in North Carolina. I went in my room and looked through our staff office numbers list.

"I'll be damned! Byron Caldwell works here." His name was fifth from the top of the page. That's why his name sounded so familiar to me. I had heard several girls talking about this fine ass teacher named Professor Caldwell. If I'm not mistaken, he teaches in the Culinary Arts Department.

A few minuets later Eric pulled up with Tracy getting out of the passenger side. Eric walked in the house first. "What's up girl?"

Tracy didn't speak to me. She just walked right past me. I started to call her out but right then I decided not to tell anybody about what I had found out. I wanted to wait and use it when I needed it. I'm gonna keep this little secret as my ace in the hole.

"Nothing. Just sitting around the house chillin'."

The next day I walked over to the Culinary Arts building to get a good look at Professor Caldwell. I went during the middle of class to make sure Tracy didn't see me over in that building. I found out what room he was in and went looking for it.

"Room thirty four, where are you?" As I turned another corner, room thirty four was directly in front of me. There was a small rectangular glass in the door. I walked up and looked in and saw the most gorgeous man I'd ever seen standing in front of the class lecturing. Byron Caldwell had the body of an ancient Greek god.

"I see why she was fucking him, that nigga fine as hell."

He had to be in his mid to late thirties, and all man. You could tell he kept himself fit. I stared through that small glass for what seemed like twenty minuets.

"May I help you young lady?"

I spun around to see that another professor had caught me looking into the class room. "No Sir. I'm fine. I was just leaving."

As I walked away from the door I figured out how to get at Ms. Thang. It was going to take a lot of work and planning but I can pull it off.

I walked out of the building and saw my little friend, Prentice, walking across campus. "Prentice hold up"

He stopped and waited on me to catch up to him. His eyes lit up, as I got closer to him.

"Hey where are you going?" I asked

"I'm bout to go get something to eat."

"I feel you. I'm 'bout to go back to the house and make a peanut butter and jelly sandwich."

"Well if you want, you can come to lunch with me. I was going to Burger King, but we can go wherever you want."

Bingo! I knew he was going to offer. He's a nice guy. Gullible, but nice.

"Well, I'm in the mood for Chinese"

"There's a Chinese buffet up the street. I hear the food there is pretty good. We can go there if you like."

"Cool, I guess we can say this is our first date."

The biggest smile ran across his face. His chest even poked out a little.

"Yeah, I guess we can say that."

We walked over to his car. He held the passenger door open for me and closed it when I sat down. As he walked around the car I watched him in the rear view mirror. He was all excited and happy. He got in the car and I leaned over and kissed him on the cheek. That was just to make sure he was gonna pay for my meal.

"Thank you for holding my door for me."

To be honest, I had never had a guy hold open a door for me. Better yet, I never had a man pay for my meal.

"No problem. A man is supposed to hold the door for a lady."

I was wearing a tight black mini skirt with heels and a red top. I caught Prentice taking quick peeks at my thighs as we drove to the restaurant. I opened my legs a little to give a better view of my upper thighs and maybe even a hint of my thong I was wearing.

"Watch out! The light red!"

He was looking so hard at my legs we almost ran out into the middle of a busy intersection.

"I'm sorry about that. My mind was a million miles away."

"Just keep your eyes on the road for right now." I could tell he was a little embarrassed. He knew I had caught him looking between my legs.

Once inside the restaurant, our waiter was a tall fine ass Chinese guy. I always thought that all Chinese people were short and skinny but this guy was about 5'10 and looked like he worked out a little. Our eyes locked and I knew I had to have some of him a.s.a.p. He took our order and in a few seconds he came back with our drinks. He placed a napkin in front of me with something written on it: Come to the door between the bathrooms in 5 minuets. I looked up at him and he smiled. I retuned the smile with a sly yes nod. Prentice was so busy looking around he had no idea what was going on in front of him. The restaurant had large fish tanks with very exotic looking fish in them. There were chandeliers hanging from the ceiling. It looked like a really fancy ballroom. Prentice and I made small talk for the next five minutes, when I said

"I'll be right back I have to go to the rest room."

"Oh, okay."

I stood up and Prentice stood up as well as I walked away from the table. I thought, he's a real gentleman.

I walked up to the middle door and turned the knob. There was the waiter sitting on a box. I walked over to him and instantly started kissing him. I had never been with an oriental person before but I was willing to be with his fine ass. Without saying a word to me, he pulled up my skirt and pulled my thong to the side. He dropped to his knees and stuck his tongue deep inside my pussy. I sat on the box and put my legs on his shoulders. He sucked my clit while he fingered me. He was going at a frantic pace I could tell he was trying to get me off quickly. As he licked me I began rubbing my clit so I could get off quick. It wasn't three minuets and I had glazed his face with my cum. He stood up and fixed his hard dick in his pants so that it was not poking straight out. He turned to me and said, "Thank you very much. Is there anything else I can get you?"

I wanted to bust out laughing. "Yeah can you get me another napkin please, to wipe my pussy."

He handed me a towel and left the room. I walked out the room about a minute after he did. I got back to the table and Prentice asked me. "You all right? You've been gone for like ten minuets."

"I'm good. Just had to take care of some female business that's all."

He didn't say anything else about it, and neither did I. The waiter walked over to our table and asked, "Is everything alright? Can I get you anything else?"

I laughed out loud. He just walked away. For the rest of our meal I kept looking at the waiter, wanting to find a way to get him back in that little room and fuck him. By the time we finished our meal, I guess they had a change of shift and our original waiter had left for the day; I wasn't mad. I guess I can add Chinese to my list of men I've been with.

CHAPTER 8

Eric

I've waited all week for Saturday to get here. Thomas, Skye, Misa and I are getting together to work on our class project today. Our class only meets on Monday and Wednesday so I've anticipated this day for the last two days. I walked into the kitchen to get a bowl of cereal before heading to the library to meet with my classmates. Michelle was sitting to the kitchen table already enjoying a healthy breakfast of eggs, sausage, toast and grits loaded with butter and giant cup of grape Flavor Aid.

I looked at all the food she was eating. "Damn girl did you make me some too?"

She looked up at me. "Hell nah! I ain't your mama."

"I hope your ass choke on that toast," I said laughing, as I poured my cereal in a bowl. Michelle stopped eating long enough to say something that really got me to thinking.

"You ever heard the expression. What you do in the dark will soon come to light?"

"Yeah I've heard that before. Why?"

"Just wondering, that's all."

I knew there was a lot more to her asking me that. She knew something about someone, and I wanted to know what it was. "Michelle, stop trippin' and tell me what you're talking about?"

"You'll find out in due time."

I hate it when people play that kid game: I know something you don't know. I just shrugged my shoulders. "Whatever."

I don't think even Michelle can get me out of the great mood I'm in today. All I could think about was spending the day with Thomas.

I pulled up to the library. I saw Misa and Skye getting out of a red Nissan Sentra. I pulled into the space right next to them. Skye stood back and waited on me to get out of my car.

"Good morning Eric." She said to me with the sexiest voice.

I put a little bass in my voice. "Good morning how are you today?"

"I'm good. So, you ready to spend a lot of time working together?"

"I'm ready for anything."

To me that sounded like a hidden invitation to something later on. My main objective is Thomas. But, I'm not gonna turn down some easy pussy either. I ran my eyes over Skye's tight sexy body. She is about 5'7 and I'll say around 140 pounds. She has short jet black hair and an apple shaped butt. Her breasts are a perfect mouth full size. Her light complexion and that body have all the guys at school wanting to get at her.

As we walked into the Library, I saw Thomas and Misa huddled up in a corner. It didn't look like they were talking about the project at all. His hands were on her thick thighs under the table. He looked up and saw Skye and me walking over, and gently removed his hand from her leg.

Misa was a stallion herself. She was thick in all the right places. She filled out a pair of jeans nicely. I would say she was a size 14 with DD breast. She had the long hair working too. It was damn near to the top of her round butt. Those Asian eyes just made a brotha want to melt. Thomas made it clear that she was what he wanted. He laughed at all her silly jokes and paid attention to every word that fell from her lips. We sat at the table for about two and a half hours when we all decided it was time to take a break. I didn't see why we needed one; we hadn't worked on the project but for twenty minuets. The rest of the time we all flirted and talked about where we were from.

While on break, I noticed Thomas walking to the rest room. I decided that this might be a good time for me to take a look at what he was working with. In jeans he looks like he's hung like a horse, but I wanted to see the uncovered version. I waited about ten seconds and walked in the restroom behind him. He stood in front of the urinal, getting ready to handle his business. I walked up to the urinal next to him.

"Thomas, your girl Misa is fine as hell." I said trying to sound as manly as I could.

I guess it's an unwritten rule that when guys are standing at a urinal you don't turn your head and look at anybody or anything. You talk looking straight ahead while pissing. I knew he wasn't gonna look at me and that was the perfect opportunity I needed to cut my eyes over and see his massive black dick sticking out the front of his pants.

Before I could catch myself, "Good God," flew from my lips. Thomas cut his eyes over at me.

"You all right?" He asked me as he shook the last few drops of pee from his dick.

"Yeah, I was just thinking about seeing Skye naked that's all." I was nervous as hell. I thought he had caught me looking at him.

"Yeah, she is fine. But imagine Misa naked. Now that's something to say good God about." We laughed a little and he walked out the door. Wait till I get home and tell Michelle I saw Thomas's dick. She's gonna trip out.

Two steps out of the restroom, I felt somebody grab my arm. It was Skye. She had stood outside the door waiting on me to come out.

"Eric come with me. I want to show you something"

We walked upstairs to a corner barely used in the library. It was obvious she had been here before 'cause she led me right to this secluded spot. The spot was tucked away from where anybody could see you. Skye walked up to me and whispered in my ear. "I want you to fuck me."

My mouth fell open as my dick jumped to an instant erection. She ran her hand down my pants and felt how hard I was.

"Damn, feel like you don't have a problem with my request."

I gently grabbed her breasts and began to massage her nipples through her shirt. After a few seconds her nipples looked like she was walking down the frozen food section at the grocery store. They were hard and almost poking through her bra. She got down her knees and undid my pants.

"You want me to suck it baby?" She asked me rubbing me through my boxer briefs.

"Go ahead, do your thang."

She pulled my dick out and I suddenly felt her hot mouth engulf me. She started out slow making sure she coated every inch of my member with her spit. I could tell she wanted to get sloppy with it but she had to remember that we were not in my house but in the school's library. She licked all around the head of my dick. Finally, she took all of me deep down her throat. It was obvious this was not the first time she sucked a dick. This girl had skills. She did this thing, where she would have my entire dick in her mouth and she would make her tongue jump while sucking me.

I thought, I'm gonna have to try that one day.

Once she had me as hard as I was gonna get, she stood up and walked over to this small table that was in the little section we were in. She undid her jeans and revealed that she was not wearing anything under them. She leaned over the table and I knew that was my cue to join in the party. I walked up behind her grabbing her butt cheeks. I spread her butt open a little and could hear the wetness of her pussy as it opened. I slid my dick right into her. Her warm moist pussy felt great around my dick. We both tried to be as quiet as we could as I rammed into her again and again.

After a few minuets I felt her body tighten up. Her hands clenched the table as her body shook the entire table. While I pounded her all I could think about was getting Thomas into this exact position. The more I thought about him the harder I slammed into Skye. After a few more seconds I felt myself ready to explode. I pulled out of her and sprayed her butt cheeks with my warm cum. She quickly pulled her jeans up and turned around and started kissing me. As we kissed I tried to pull my pants back up and get myself situated. She looked me right in the eyes laughing.

"Damn boy, when was the last time you got some? You shot a gallon of that shit on me."

I tried not to laugh too hard. "It's been a little while."

"Well I hope we can do it again really soon. But next time, I want to be in your bed."

I thought, she got another thang coming if she think I'm ever gonna have her over funking up my sheets.

We walked back down stairs to the table where we were all sitting. I noticed that Thomas and Misa had left. Misa left Skye a note on her book pack:

Skye,
Thomas and I are going back to his place to work on our own little project. I'll see you later.

Misa

Skye turned to me. "I guess you'll have to take me home. Misa and Thomas left."

"No problem. Let's go."

I really wanted to knock her upside her head. Because of her hot in the pants ass, I missed an opportunity to work on Thomas a little more.

On the way to Skye's house she kept rubbing my leg. I wanted to smack her hand every time she touched me but I was trying to be nice. I walked her to her door.

"Would you like to come in for a while?" She asked, looking at me like she wanted to pull me in.

"Nah, I have to take my roommate to work in a few. And, I don't want her to be late."

"You live with that chunky girl Michelle don't you?"

"Yeah. Why?" I knew something was said about us living together at that point.

"No reason just asking. Y'all are just roommates right?"

"Yes."

"Well maybe you can tell me why her attitude is so jacked up. Is she like that at home?"

"Don't talk about my girl. She cool and that's all you need to know about her. Now I have to go." With that I turned and walked away. How dare she talk about one of my friends! But, she was telling the truth, Michelle does need to slow that funky attitude down a little bit.

When I got back home, Tracy was sitting on the porch looking like she had just lost her favorite dog.

"Damn girl, why the long face?"

"It's Brandon. He's acting a little funny all of a sudden."

I walked over and sat next to her on the porch. "Baby look…" Just then my cell started to ring. I looked at the caller I.D. and got right back up.

I looked at Tracy "I have to take this call. We'll talk a little later."

I stood up and walked toward the front door.

"Hey, wuz up B?"

CHAPTER 9

Tracy

I hate Tuesdays and Thursdays. Those are the days I have to go to Byron's class. After our last run in, I've tried to avoid him when I see him on campus. Today I can't run; I have to go sit in his classroom. I can only hope that class will be canceled by the time I get there.

As I walked across campus to the culinary building I saw Michelle coming from the student union. We walked directly towards one another. I'm not gonna move, and if she so much as brushes up against me, I'm gonna jump on her big ass. Our eyes locked on one another. My heart started beating faster and faster the closer we got. I can't believe it. In the middle of campus we are about to settle our little problem. I clenched my fist ready to throw the first punch, when she said, "Hey Tracy how are you today?"

I know I have the stupidest look on my face right about now. My words got caught up in my throat. I didn't know what to say. I was ready to start swinging and cursing. She stood and looked at me like we were old friends. Finally, I managed to get a few words out.

"Hey wuz up?" I still had my fist clenched. Michelle is the type of girl that would try to sucka punch you when you least expect it. I wasn't gonna put my guard down. I was still ready for anything. Michelle had a very pleasant look on her face. Her voice was actually high pitched and cheerful.

"It's all good. I really want us to bury the hatchet. We have to live in that house together and there is no need in us making our own living arrangements harder than they have to be. So, I want to call a truce."

I just stood there and stared at her for a second or two. I thought, who does she think she's foolin'. That bitch ain't got a happy bone in her body. She's up to something. I just have to pay attention and wait to find out what it is. But for now I'll play her little game. "Okay Michelle, truce. Let's just start over and let bygones be bygones."

We both kinda smiled at one another and walked away. I kept turning around to see if she was running up behind me trying to hit me in the head or something.

The closer I got to the Culinary building, the sicker my stomach began to feel. The sick feeling reminded me of when I was in high school, not wanting to get off the school bus at my exit because I knew I had a bad report card. The closer I got to home, the worse I felt. I walked into the building with about 2 minutes to spare before the start of class. Normally I walk slow, dreading going to this class, but today I walked extra slow hoping that by the time I got to the class door it would be locked. Byron had a habit of locking students out of class if they were late, and would not give them the work they missed.

I looked at my watch. "2:47, I'm two minutes late and I know he has locked the door. I might as well go to the house."

Almost instantly, the sick feeling went away. I turned around in the hallway and started to walk away when I heard Byron's voice. "Tracy! I was just about to lock the door. Good thing I decided to look out and see if anybody else was on the way to class. Come on in."

Like magic, the sick feeling reappeared. I began my death march to the last row in class. I sat behind the biggest guy in school. I didn't want Byron to see or remember that I was there. Class went on and I sat in the back hardly seen and as quiet as I could be. I kept looking at my watch hoping the time was almost up for class. About 30 minuets into class Byron decided to end class. All the students jumped up and left before he had a chance to change his mind. My bag was on my shoulder and my feet were carrying me as fast as they could to the door when Byron spoke to me.

"Tracy, don't leave just yet. I have a few things to go over with you."

I knew damn well there was nothing he had to go over with me. This was just another attempt to get me alone with him. I looked around to see if any of the other students were still leaving. As soon as I looked at the door the last guy walked out. It was Byron and I alone again. He walked over to me with that cocky swagger of his. Back in Miami, that walk of his used to turn me on. Now it turns my stomach. Soon as he parted his lips to talk to me I knew nothing good was about to hit my ears.

"How about you and I together for dinner tonight."

I looked at him like he was crazy. "No that's okay."

"That was not a question. I'm telling you, I'm taking you to dinner tonight. We need to be away from here to talk about our relationship."

"What relationship! I don't like you. I made a mistake before, and I'm not making it again!"

"That's where you and I differ. You call it a mistake; I call it sending your parents a tape of us in Miami fucking on my patio.

I felt my mouth drop open.

"From the look on your face, I can tell that you forgot about our wild and consensual night. But I remember it like it was yesterday. Hell, as a matter of fact, I watched that tape yesterday."

Anger consumed me. I was mad enough to spit fire. I wanted to scratch his eyes from his face. Venom spewed from my mouth as I spoke. "You lying muthafucka! You don't have a damn tape of anything. Your ass is too ashamed to show your little ass dick. So, I know you didn't film shit!"

"Okay, if I'm lying, walk out that door and see if I don't send your family and your boyfriend's family a copy!"

In my heart I felt as if he didn't have a tape and I was willing to try and call his bluff. I grabbed up my things and walked towards the door. My mind raced, trying to figure out if there was a night that I was drunk and he could have filmed me. I was coming up with nothing. So, I knew he was full of shit. I reached for the door handle and Byron called my name.

"Tracy, remember that night we went to The Red Light."

I stopped just short of the door. I do remember going to

that club. It's a very trendy nightspot in Miami. If you want to go party in Miami, that's the place to go. We did have a great time that night.

"That was the night you told me that you loved me and I was proud to say that I loved you."

I turned to him. "Byron, why do you want to hurt me like this?"

I had to play the sincere hurt woman to try to get him to back off me a little bit.

"I didn't want it to come to me bringing that tape up but I'm tired of you trippin' every time we see each other. I just want things to go back to the way they were between us."

"But things have changed. I'm engaged now."

"So, I don't want to marry you. I just want to hit it, from time to time. I could care less about you getting married to Brandon. As a matter of fact, where are you registered, so I can go ahead and get ya'll a little something."

The thought of him all over me again depressed me. I don't know what I was thinking when we got together. But now I'm between a rock and a hard place. "What time should I be ready for dinner, and where are we going?"

He looked at me with a nasty grin on his face. "Now was that so hard?" He asked me as he walked over to me and rubbed my hair. "Be ready at seven o'clock. Where I'm taking you is a surprise."

I gave him a fake smile and walked out the classroom. The last thing I wanted to do was get right back into the same bad situation I tried to leave behind. But I had no other choice.

If Byron really has a tape of me, I can't let my family or Brandon's family find out in such a way. Brandon's family would be crushed. He and I have been together for such a long time. His father is a Minister at a Baptist Church back home and he said God told him Brandon and I was meant for each other. And, to be honest, to this day I believe him. But I guess all it took was one fight between Brandon and I and I was off in another man's arms.

I don't really remember what the fight was about, but I do remember being very upset during one of Byron's classes last year.

He asked me what was wrong and I just started talking. Before I realized it, he and I had talked for almost three hours. I had never been able to just sit down and talk to Brandon. He's the type that doesn't want to hear your problem, he wants to fix it. This was new to me. An older man that listened to me. I was used to guys my age that thought they knew everything but really had no clue what was going on around them. At the time I was 20 and Byron was 36. I always thought I was too mature for guys my age. But my age is actually what got me into this mess. He knew exactly what to say to a twenty-year-old woman, but I had no clue what a 36-year-old man really wanted from me. It just made me feel good to be able to have this older guy chase me. We went to the finest restaurants in town. He showered me with gifts and constantly told me how beautiful I am. My head was as big as a fifteen-passenger van. I knew I was the shit on campus. If he thought I was upset with him about something, he went to the limit to find out what the problem was and try to fix it. I was in heaven, or so I thought.

The first time we had sex, it was phenomenal. He ate me for what seemed like an hour. He made sure I got off several times by his tongue before we had intercourse. Brandon always said I'm not eating anything you pee out of. But it was always okay for me to suck him off. Byron had no problem with going down on me. The first time we actually made love it was full of passion. He held me close to him during our escapade. His hands touched every inch of my body. He made sure I had several orgasms before he did. He made me feel like a real woman. Afterwards we would lie together and just talk about any and everything.

Several times Brandon asked me if I was seeing someone else because I was acting like I really didn't care about him anymore, and it was showing. I was ready to tell Brandon it was over between us when Byron started being the Byron I know now. One night he asked me to go to dinner with him but I already had plans to go out with Brandon. He flipped out on me, called me everything but a child of God; told me that I was acting like a little girl and that he should have known better to get involved with a child. He went on and on. I decided right then to get out of this relationship with him.

I didn't want to return to class and I was lucky that all of this went on almost at the end of the semester. I went to class every now and then just enough to stay on top of what was going on. I stopped seeing him and he became obsessed with trying to get me back into his life. It got to the point where I knew if I stayed at that college he would just hound me and pester me the entire time. I put in for my transfer to another college. He overheard me telling a friend that I was leaving school and I guess he pulled my records and found out where I was going and came here also. Now I have to find a way to end this game with him for good.

Thank God nobody was home when Byron came to pick me up at seven. He blew the horn to let me know he was outside, waiting. As I got in his car, I could see him looking at me with that nasty lust in his eyes. It almost made me sick to my stomach. "So Byron, where are we going?" I asked, hoping it would be somewhere out of town.

"Don't worry princess; you will be treated like royalty tonight."

We drove for about 15 minutes, and then he pulled up to a townhouse across town. He parked the car and opened the door for me. I slowly walked with him into the house. The aroma of Italian food hit me as soon as I walked in. The lights were dimmed low and Luther was playing on the sound system. This would have been a romantic setting if I were with someone I loved, but the thought of being alone with Byron made me nervous.

"Have a seat, while I plate up the food."

"Where's your restroom?" I asked, hoping this night would end quickly.

"Down the hall, last room on your right." He replied. Byron went to the kitchen to get dinner ready. When I returned, he already had the food on the table. He remembered my favorite dish, seafood Alfredo, breadsticks, and salad with Italian dressing. He poured two glasses of white wine, and sat down across from me.

Byron commented throughout dinner on how beautiful I was and how he remembered all the wonderful nights we spent together. I must admit, it was wonderful. Byron always made me feel like a woman.

"Byron, we did have good times, but that was all a mistake. I love Brandon, and I will be his wife soon. I wish you would just leave the past in the past."

"Like I told you before Tracy, I don't care who you love or marry, but that pussy belongs to me. As long as you cooperate with me, Brandon's parents will never have to see their sweet innocent future daughter-in-law getting fucked in the ass by another man. Besides, you weren't thinking about him before when you were lying up in my bed with your legs spread. What's the difference now?"

Tears ran down my face as I looked at him in disbelief. How did I ever get myself involved in this situation? I thought Byron cared about me, but now I see he only wants self-gratification. But what I can't understand is, why me? Byron is very handsome and can have any woman he wants. If Byron has this so-called video of me, I know I have to do whatever he wants, so I can marry Brandon.

Byron left me there crying and got up and walked to the back of the house. When he got back, he was butt ass naked. His manhood was semi-erect. He grabbed my hand and led me to his bedroom. Candles were lit around the room, and pink and red rose petals were lying on the bed. He told me to take my clothes off, but I stood there and hesitated. He walked over and turned on his 42-inch plasma T.V.

My reality immediately flashed on the screen. There I was… making love to Byron. Horrified, I started to unbutton my blouse and Byron walked over and led me to the bed. As my blouse fell to the floor he was kissing my chest. His tongue felt like a snakes, the way it darted out of his mouth as he licked me. I wanted to cry but I didn't want to give him the satisfaction of fucking me and seeing me cry at the same time. He laid me on the bed and rubbed my entire body. He knelt between my legs and started to lick me. Normally any woman can get past any feelings as long as a man has his tongue in her, but with Byron it was different. I wanted to puke. I looked over at the television and saw myself riding his dick. He must have seen me looking at it.

"You like watching yourself huh?"

I didn't answer.

"You might as well enjoy it like you did before. Remember how you use to yell, fuck me Byron, harder. That's what I want you to say tonight. I like a woman that can talk dirty while she's fucking."

He climbed on top of me and slid his dick into me as far as it would go. I hadn't been with anybody for a few months and I was a little tight. He didn't waste any time going right to work. There was no caressing or rubbing. It was, I'm on and I'm gonna beat the hair off of it. He pounded me like a man possessed.

"Come on Tracy say it. Tell me to fuck you harder!"

"Okay Fuck you Byron. Fuck you harder!"

He was so into it he didn't realize what I had actually said.

"Fuck you baby. Come on fuck you!" It was actually a little funny to me. He was pumping for all he was worth and I was cursing him out, and laughing about it.

"Come on Tracy. Bend over and let me hit it from the back!"

I turned over and put my butt high in the air. He got behind me and started pounding again. This was the first time in my life I wanted to actually fart on a man during sex. If I could have squeezed one out I would have. That's how much I hate this bastard. A few seconds in this position and he was ready to cum.

"Yeah Tracy I'm gonna cum all over you tight little ass!" He pointed his dick directly at me and let it fly. His cum splattered all over my butt and back. I felt so dirty. All I could do was jump up and run to the bathroom. I grabbed his face towel and cleaned my butt with it, and folded it back up nicely and put it back where I found it. He came to the door.

"Now was that so bad. That reminded me of the old times we had together."

I didn't bother to answer him. He just kept talking.

"You know it would have been better if you had gotten into it a little more. That was always a problem with you. You're always so uptight. Chill out a little."

If I had a gun, I'd shoot him square in the ass. I snatched

open the bathroom door. "Can you take me home now please?"

"Yeah I guess so. Come on, get dressed. I have a busy day tomorrow."

After all that now the nigga wants to rush me. But, that's fine the quicker I get dressed the quicker I'm out of his nasty ass house.

On the way home, he wanted to make small talk. I didn't care to say another word to him. All I could think about was Brandon. I love him so much. He's my everything. I would kill myself if he ever found out about Byron.

CHAPTER 10

Michelle

For the next few days I went out of my way to be nice to Tracy. I invited her to watch a movie I had rented. When I went out to get something to eat I asked if I could bring her back anything. It took a few days to get her to trust me, but soon she was just where I wanted her. We are actually talking to one another like old girlfriends. She is even telling me about niggas she thinks fine. Deep down inside I still hate that bitch. I have something in store for Ms. Thang. She has no clue what's coming in her direction.

This morning I heard Tracy in the kitchen, rummaging through the cabinets, looking for something for breakfast. I walked into the kitchen "Tracy, if you drive I'll buy us breakfast at Hardee's, my treat."

No matter what complexion she is, a nigga is still a nigga, and we don't pass up the opportunity for a free meal.

"Yeah, let's go. Thanks."

It was my first time in Tracy's car. I must admit, it was tight. The leather interior was off the hook and the sound system was bangin'. I noticed she has a picture of her boyfriend Brandon taped to the dashboard. Since that night I first met him at the party I often think about him.

I made a little conversation on the way to get our food. "So, this is your boyfriend right?"

"Yeah, that's my boo, Brandon."

Her face turned red and a smile went from ear to ear just talking about him. She has no idea my goal is to sleep with him. "How long have ya'll been together?"

"About six or seven years. We've been together, seems like forever."

"He's back in Miami right?"

"Yeah."

"You must have a lot of trust in him. Being down there with all those beautiful women and all."

"I trust him. We've been through a lot together."

"Girl you're a good one. I don't trust no man. All of them will fuck anything with a pussy!" All I need to do is get that one speck of doubt in her man and I got her hooked.

"Brandon's not like that. He's a one-woman man. He's been mine and only mine since we've been together. Our families love one another and we might as well be planning our wedding day. It's pretty much written in stone that we will be together forever."

"Let me ask you this then. Have you ever done anything to him that crushed him and he forgave you for it?"

Tracy got quiet. I know what the answer is, but I want her to remember what she did and get her to start thinking about the possibility of Brandon cheating. After taking a deep breath she finally answered, "Yeah, but that was a while ago. We're past that now."

"Girl, they are never past some shit that hurt them. They will make you think that they are cool with it, and all is good, but trust me, they will try to get you back later down the road."

A sick look fell across her face. I know I have her. The doubt is there and I can see the gears in her head working. She is thinking about that shit she pulled back in Miami with Byron. I didn't know it would be so much fun messing with her head. I thought she would be a tough nut to crack, but she was easy, very easy.

We pulled up to the Hardee's on 5th street, and ordered our food. She hadn't said another word about Brandon since I planted the seed of doubt in her head. We talked about everything under the sun but him. I decided to leave the Brandon situation alone for the moment. She looked like she was ready to cry every time she looked at his picture on the dash. A few minutes later she asked me a question.

"I heard you were up in the guys' dorm a while back."

"Yeah, I was in there handling my business."

"From what I heard you handled more than just your business."

"What do you mean?"

"I heard you slept with six guys at the same time. That's the story that's going 'round."

Damn she's sitting here trying to turn the tables on me. Trying to get me to talk about who and what I did. "Nah, it wasn't like that at all. You know nigga's always lying on their dicks. But I heard you have a little crush on a professor?"

Suddenly the car swerved a little. She frantically pulled into a grocery store parking lot. "What are you talking about? What did you hear!"

I almost jumped out the car. She scared the hell out of me. Her eyes were bulging out of her head. She had a grip on the steering wheel. The veins on the side of her face had become visible.

"Damn girl I was just trippin! I ain't heard shit." The way she reacted just proved to me that something between her and Professor Caldwell is still going on. I'm going to make it my business to find out what it is. I don't want to use all my cards I'm playing with right now, so I'm gonna back off that hot topic. My plan for her just got bigger and better. At first I just wanted to fuck her man and humiliate her, but now I can damn near destroy her silly stuck up ass.

We pulled out of the parking lot and I asked her to drop me off on campus. On the way there I wanted to find out a little more about Brandon and finish messing with her head a little. I asked her, "So what did you do?"

"What are you talking about?"

"When you hurt Brandon. What did you do to hurt him?"

"I cheated on him"

"You don't look like the cheating type."

"What does the cheating type look like?" she said with a little smirk on her face.

"You know what I mean. You all prissy and stuff. You look like the stay at home and have a bunch of babies while the husband goes to work and fuck his secretary type."

We both laughed a little then she started talking. "Well, I've always seen myself as that type, but this one guy showed me, there is more to life than sitting at home waiting on my man to come in."

I sat and listened to her go on and on about this other guy. It sounded like she had fallen in love with him. When she was finished I asked her a few of my own questions.

"So you really believe that Brandon just forgave you for all that happened?"

"Yes."

"Then you're out of your damn mind. That nigga ain't forgave shit. Tell me this. Have you ever called him and he seemed too busy to talk to you?"

She looked confused. I asked another question before she had the opportunity to answer the first one. "Have you called him and he talked to you but rushed you off the phone? Or better yet, have you called him and somebody else answered the phone?"

Her eyes went glassy. She looked like she was struggling to hold back tears. I put the icing on the cake with my last comment.

"If you can answer yes to any of those questions, then your man might be cheating on you."

She never said another word in the car till we got to the campus. "Where do you want me to drop you off at?" She asked, her voice trembling.

"Right here in front will be fine. I see somebody I need to holla at." I got out of the car and we said our goodbyes and Tracy pulled off. I waited till she was around the corner and busted out laughing. I was all in her head. I could tell by the look in her face she didn't know what to think.

I sat on a bench and pulled my food out the bag when I saw this fine ass white boy walking by. The white boy was built like a brotha. He had the thick cut arms and the high tight butt. I wanted some of him in a bad way. As he walked by me I started talking to him.

"Hey you, sit down and talk to me for a while." He turned

and looked at me as if he was surprised I was actually talking to him. I continued, "So what's your name?"

As he walked over and began to sit down he answered, "Steve."

"Nice to meet you Steve. I'm Michelle"

I noticed him looking at my thick thighs and well-manicured toes. I was wearing a jean mini and a low cut blouse. My mother always told me to look good when I walk out the house because I never knew who I was going to meet. Today I had no intentions of trying to get with anybody but Steve was too fine to pass up.

"So, Steve I hear that country boy accent. Where are you from?

"Williamston, North Carolina."

"That's not too far from here is it?"

"No, it's about forty five minuets or so."

From what I had heard Williamston was a small rural town. It only has one high school and the biggest thing there is the local Wal-Mart. But, I also heard that the guys from there love to fuck and I was gonna find out in a few.

"Do you live here on campus?"

"No, I have an apartment not too far from here."

"I would love to see it sometime." He looked at me; I guess he was not ready for my forwardness.

"Well actually, I have a class in about an hour. I was just going to the weight room to get a quick work out but…"

"Let's work out together back at your place."

We got up and we walked back to his car. He drove a 1999 Dodge Dakota Sport. It was okay but at that moment he could have drove a lime green Gremlin and I would not have cared. We pulled out of the parking lot. At the first red light we got to Prentice pulled up next to us. I tried to duck down in the car but it was too late, he was looking at me trying to hide. I glanced over and waved as the light turned green. He looked shocked. As we turned a corner my cell phone rang. I looked at the caller I.D. and it was Prentice. I didn't answer the phone. He called repeatedly and I never answered. Steve looked at me

"Somebody sure wants to talk to you bad."

"Yeah, it's this guy I've been trying to get rid of."

Moments later we pulled up to his apartment. It was a very nice place. The lawn was well kept and, surprisingly, the elevator here worked. We went up to the third floor of the building. His apartment was the last one on the left. He opened the door and my mouth fell open. His place was hooked up. He had the black leather furniture with a thirty-six inch high definition TV. The beige carpet was spotless and he even had nice art on the walls. I was use to that old picture of three dogs playing cards or the pictures of two black people lying naked embracing one another. I was shocked. I just knew when I got there he would have old dirty dishes stacked up on the floor and the place would smell like a wet dog. There was no spider lamps or liquor bottles lining the top of the entertainment center. This white boy actually had a little bit of class.

We sat on the sofa and talked a little more, he was telling me about Williamston. I could care less about all of that. We were short on time and I wanted to fuck. As he was talking I leaned over and shoved my tongue into his mouth. Automatically his hands wrapped around my ass. I straddled him as we kissed. His hands went under my skirt and squeezed my cheeks.

"Yeah that's it squeeze this fat black ass." He did what he was told. I took his shirt off and ran my tongue down his chest. His pink nipples were hard and from where I was sitting his dick was even harder. He pulled my breast out through the top of my low cut blouse. He sucked my hard nipples as I became wetter and wetter by the second. I stood up and slid my skirt off. His eyes widened as he saw me standing in front of him in my red lace thong. I propped one leg up on the sofa and commanded "Come lick this chocolate kitty."

He fell to his knees and without hesitation pulled my thong to the side and began licking my slit like a cat lapping milk from a dish. I grabbed the back of his head and shoved him as far into my pussy as possible. His tongue felt like it was a mile long. He was licking spots that had never been licked. A few seconds later I glazed his face with my juices. He stood up and dropped his jeans.

To my surprise he wasn't wearing any underwear. That old saying that white men all have small dicks went right out the window. Steve was hung. His dick looked like it belonged on a male stripper. He would have made any sistah take notice. I grabbed his dick with one hand and gobbled him up. My head bounced back and forth as his blond pubic hairs tickled my nose. I was having the time of my life. I had never been with a white guy before and have never really been attracted to them but there was something about Steve that was different. He was white but had everything that the finest brotha I've ever been with had, including a big dick.

Steve turned me around. I knew he wanted to fuck me from the back. He had to wonder what it was like to fuck a big butt black woman and he finally got his chance. I bent over, showing him right where to insert his manhood. I felt him inch his way into me. It felt good being filled like that. He grabbed my hips and began thrusting into me. I was sent right over the edge from the first stroke. I was cumming all over him. The wet sound of him slamming into my sopping pussy was turning me on even more. My large tits swung back and forth as he fucked me doggy style. I came a few more times and he still had not cum for me.

He took his dick out and asked me, "Let me fuck your ass?"

I was so horny I said yes without even thinking. His dick was so wet from my pussy he didn't need any other lubrication to go inside my backdoor. The head of his dick stretched me. I felt a little pain but he slowed down and took his time. Slowly he entered me. Finally he was all the way in. he gave me a few short strokes just to get me into it.

"Come on baby fuck this big ass!" I yelled.

He started pounding me. It felt great having him up my ass. He grabbed a hand full of my hair. I wanted to turn around and knock his ass out for touching my hair but that would have meant letting his dick out of my ass and I didn't want that. Normally I love having a man pull my hair, but I just got back from the salon yesterday. It all felt too good, so I let it go. He pulled my hair as he fucked me. I felt submissive. His strokes became faster. I knew he was finally ready to cum. He pulled his dick from my ass and sprayed my back with his white hot cum. My ass hole was wide open and I felt a few drops got in. That was a major turn on. He walked over to the closet and gave me a towel. "You can take a shower if you like."

"Thank you, I think I need to." I went into his bathroom. Me being me, I opened the medicine cabinet. He had a gold rope chain laying on one of the shelves. I closed the door and took my shower. As I was drying off I opened the cabinet door again and took the chain out of it. I closed it in my hand and put it in my pocket as I put back on my skirt. I thought, did he think I was gonna come over here and let him fuck my ass for free. He owes me this chain. He was sitting on the sofa watching me get dressed.

I hope you enjoyed yourself." He said, reaching out to rub my butt.

"I had a great time. I hope we can do this again real soon."

"Me too."

We walked back to his car and drove back to campus. He dropped me off in front of the building where my next class was and he drove off. I began to walk inside the building when I heard someone screaming

"Michelle!"

I turned and it was Prentice walking up really fast towards me.

"Why the fuck are you calling me like that?"

"I know you had your phone on. I was calling you earlier."

"Yeah, and? What do you want?"

"Who was that white boy?"

"First of all don't ever walk up on me again asking me questions! Secondly, none of your damn business who that white boy was! Last, if you ever try to embarrass me again, I'll fuck you up, you hear me!"

People had stopped and were looking at us. The look on his face told me he was ready to crawl under a rock. I had told him off in front of everybody in the building. He looked at me with the puppy dog eyes.

"I'm sorry. It's just that I thought you and I were dating and I got a little crazy when I saw you with him and you wouldn't answer your phone."

A few guys started laughing when he apologized. I noticed a few girls were looking at him with disgust. I had punked him.

"Look, you're my boy and I love spending time with you, but you have to trust me. I'm not doing anything to mess up what we have."

"Does that mean we're a couple?"

"No, that means I like you a lot." He seemed satisfied with my answer. I guess he had no choice but to be.

CHAPTER 11

Eric

The three members of my study group and I decided it would be better if the guys worked together and the girls worked together, and just meet to go over everything one day on the weekend. I'm fine with that 'cause it gives Thomas and I a little guy time. Most of the time Thomas and I are together we are talking about women. But today was a little different. As we sat to the table in his apartment he looked at me. "Eric, I have a question for you."

"Go ahead."

"It's a well known fact that you are a bi-sexual man right?"

"Yeah, I don't try to hide it. Why?" I was hoping that this conversation was going to lead to me fucking him.

"Well, my question is, how do you bring yourself to suck another man's dick. I'm not trying to disrespect you or anything but I think I would throw up if I touched another man's dick, let alone sucked it."

I sat there for a moment. That's not what I thought he was going to say, but I had to give him an answer.

"Well, just like eating a pussy. They piss out of it and lord knows what else they do with it. But, that has never stopped you from going down there getting a mouth full has it? It's the same with sucking a dick. We piss out of it and quick to stick it in somebody's mouth. Besides, take my word on this. A man is the best dick sucker on the planet, trust me. You know how they say women eat pussy better than men? Well, it's the same thing for guys."

Thomas looked like he was ready to throw up by me just

talking about it. So I furthered the conversation. "So you mean to tell me that you never in your life ever thought about being with another man?"

"Hell no!" His voice rang all over the apartment.

"Well all I have to say is, don't knock it till you've try it"

"I'll knock the hell out of somebody if they even approach me with that silly shit."

"Now why it got to be all that. Just say no I don't get down like that and let it be. Don't go beating up people for it."

His last comment pissed me off. I had to speak my mind at this point. "That's what's wrong with straight people: they always want to jump up and hit somebody for approaching you. One day one of ya'll is gonna mess around and hit the wrong gay guy, and get your ass beat. Just because we're gay or bi don't mean we're not men. We'll still beat that ass if need be."

Thomas looked at me and busted out laughing, "Damn dawg, you a trip you know that?"

We changed the topic and continued to work on our project. Midway through our work, my cell phone rang.

"Hello?"

"Hey sexy!"

"B, what's going on man?"

"I'm good. Look, I'll be up that way this Friday."

"Really! Damn, I look forward to seeing you again. I miss you." I looked over at Thomas and his face was damn near green. He knew I was talking to a guy.

"I miss you too. I'm gonna be staying at the Ramada Inn on Arlington while I'm there."

"That's cool. Just call me when it's a good time for me to visit."

"Shall do."

"Aiight."

"Bye."

I hung up the phone and the biggest smile was on my face. Thomas looked at me then asked, "So I take it your man is coming to see you soon?"

"Yeah he's coming this weekend"

"Gonna get that good head huh?" he said laughing.

"I don't know. We haven't slept together yet."

A few hours later I was home with Michelle. I walked into her bedroom. She was laying across the bed in nothing but a bra and panties.

"Wuz up Michelle. How was your day?"

"It was cool. Got mine with a white boy but the best thing was I punked my boy Prentice for trying to show out on me."

"I don't know why you won't leave that little man alone. He's the type that will get emotionally involved and fuck you up if shit don't turn out the way he want it to."

"I'll beat his ass, he try to run up on me."

I sat down on the bed next to Michelle. She looked into my eyes and knew I was excited about something. "So are you gonna tell me?" She said sitting up exposing her large, lace-cupped breast.

"You know me too damn good. My boy B is coming this weekend."

"Your boy B?"

"Yeah he's this new guy I've been talking to lately."

"Where is he coming from?"

"Miami."

Just then I heard Tracy coming through the door. She ran to Michelle's room.

"Oh my bad, I didn't know you were in here Eric. But I'm glad you're here. I have great news!"

Michelle and I both sat straight up to make sure we heard everything she was about to say.

"Brandon is coming up here Saturday. I told you Michelle, we're past all of that old stuff. I asked him to come and he said yes without even questioning it."

I stood back with a smile on my face.

"That's good. Eric has a friend coming to town this weekend. Maybe we all can hang out at the club."

Tracy jumped in. "We don't normally do clubs but I think we can change up our routine for one night."

Right then I knew that night would be a very

uncomfortable night for me. I walked out of the room. I went into the kitchen for something to drink. As I closed the door Tracy was standing there and scared the hell out of me.

"Girl, don't be standing behind doors like that!"

"I'm sorry but you seem like something's on your mind"

"I'm cool. It's just…I don't know. Can I ask you a question?"

"Sure, go ahead."

"Have you ever hurt an innocent friend?"

She sat for a second then answered. "What's the deal with you and Michelle both asking me these type of questions today? But, to answer you, no, I've never hurt an innocent friend. I have hurt a boyfriend before, but not a person I considered my friend. Why, who is doing you wrong?"

I just looked at her and shook my head "It's not me that's being done wrong."

"You want to talk about it?"

"Nah, not right now."

As I turned and walked away. Part of me is hurting on the inside because I know a friend that is gonna go off the deep end when a secret I'm keeping comes to light. The other part of me is beyond happy because my friend is coming this Friday and it's going to be our first time together. I haven't felt like this since my first sexual experience. I have butterflies in my stomach just thinking about it.

It's Friday morning and I woke up around 6:15 a.m. I normally don't get up till around 11:00 a.m. on Friday 'cause I don't have any classes that day. But excitement woke me up this morning. I was up before anybody else in the house. As pretty and prissy as Tracy is, that girl snores like a grown man. Sometimes I can hear her through her closed door at night. But that's my girl and I'm not gonna put the bad mouth on her. I guess the smell of bacon, eggs, and grits woke Tracy up. I'm cooking me a good breakfast 'cause I know I'm going to need my strength later. Tracy walked in and sat to the kitchen table while I cooked. She started a conversation I really don't feel like having today.

"What got you up so early?"

"I'm getting ready for a big day with my friend"

"That's right your boy is coming in today right?"

"Yeah, I'm a little excited."

I almost dropped my food on the floor with her next statement.

"I think something is going on with Brandon."

I stopped in mid stride of cooking. I was standing with my back to her cause I knew if she could look at my face she would question me to death. I have to act like nothing's wrong.

"What's up with him?"

"I tried to call him a little while ago and he's not answering his phone. And, that's not like him."

"Just because he's not answering his phone, something's wrong with him? You need to stop trippin'."

"You right. I think it's that conversation Michelle and I had the other day that's got me some mixed up."

"What conversation?"

"She was asking me have I ever hurt him and if so, do I think he really forgave me. Or is he just picking his time to get me back. Stuff like that."

Right then I wanted to go wake Michelle's ass up. She's up to something; I just don't know what it is.

"Don't pay Michelle any attention. She's always been in fucked up relationships and if you listen to her yours will be just as fucked up."

We both laughed a little and dropped the topic. I felt horrible trying to make her feel good about her man that I've been secretly talking to and going to hook up with in a few hours. The saddest part of the entire situation is that Michelle is right. I know that Brandon, or B as I like to call him, is still hurting on the inside about something that went down between him and Tracy. He doesn't want to talk about it and I don't push the issue.

For the rest of the morning and the early afternoon, I watched as Tracy tried to call Brandon's phone over and over again. She is starting to get on my nerves calling him so much. I walked into my bedroom and closed the door and called him from my cell. He picked up on the first ring.

"Hello?"

"Hey boo, how's the trip so far?"

"It's good. I should be there in about forty-five minutes. I'm driving a red Nissan Altima fully loaded."

"Has Tracy been calling you this morning?"

"Yeah, she's been blowing my phone up all morning!"

"Look you need to call her and tell her your cell battery is dead or something 'cause she was talking to our other roommate and she has put all kinds of thoughts in Tracy's head about you still being hurt and gonna try to hurt her in return."

"You talking about that fat girl Michelle?"

"Yes."

"All right! I'll call Tracy now okay?"

"Good. I'll see you when you get here."

As I hung up the phone and walked back into the front room where Tracy was I could hear her cell phone start ringing in her bedroom. She jumped up and ran to her room. Once she realized it was Brandon she closed the door to her room.

Looking at the clock it's now 2:30. My excitement is hard to hide. Several times Michelle has asked me to sit down and stop pacing back and forth across the room. I walked into my room to make sure I had packed up all my little toys and accessories. I made sure I had my Astroglide, my size four Anal Plug, my 10 inch Anal Beads and I can't have a good time without my Pina Colada Motion Lotion. I grabbed my bags and headed for the door. I was stopped by Tracy walking out of her room. Her face was wet from tears. I had to be a good friend and ask, "What's wrong baby?" I said with my most concerned voice.

"It's Brandon. He rushed me off the phone and said he had to run inside whatever place he's at. He said he'll call me back in a few hours. "

Just then Michelle jumped into the conversation. "I told you, didn't I? I told you when they start rushing you off the phone and acting like they don't have time for you anymore they're up to no damn good!"

I screamed, "Michelle shut the fuck up! You don't have a

clue what you're talking about! Maybe the guy actually has something to do and can't talk at this moment."

Michelle chimed in with another one of her sarcastic answers. "Yeah, or somebody else to do!"

I wanted to snatch Michelle's lips off to make her stop talking. I'm trying my best to look out for my girls' feelings and she's sitting there filling her head with a ton of bullshit. I shot Michelle a shut the hell up look. She looked at me and frowned up her face as I exited the room.

I turned and looked at Tracy. "Girl, it'll be okay, trust me. Don't give that shit Michelle talking a second thought. You have a good man that loves you. Remember that."

Tracy just kinda sat there on the sofa and stared at me as I left the house. I wanted to feel bad, but I couldn't. I was too excited about meeting Brandon in a few minutes.

Turning into the parking lot of the hotel, I saw Brandon's red Nissan Altima. It had gray leather seats and his car also had the Bose speakers everybody wants in their car. I looked in the rear view mirror to make sure I was on point. My hair was fine, my face was not to shiny from the lotion I had on. I am looking good I must admit. Walking into the main lobby of the hotel I felt like all eyes were on me. Everybody seemed to stop and stare when I walked in. Brandon was standing at the check in desk when I walked up behind him. "Hey sexy!"

He turned around to see who was calling somebody sexy all loud. His face almost fell to the floor when he turned and saw that the loud person was me. The young lady behind the desk looked at both of us. I guess she thought one of us was gonna holla at her but we had other plans. Her world looked wrecked when I walked up and gave Brandon a huge hug. Brandon pushed me away from him. I'm thinking I know this nigga ain't trippin' on me. He better know that I don't play with all the pushin' shit. The look on his face was pure disgust as he held me at arms length. He finally spoke to me. "Wuz up dawg!"

I was confused. I thought he would have been more excited to see me. The bitch in me is on its way out. Then it hit me. Brandon is not as open as I am. I don't care if people know that

I'm bi, but he does care. And, I have to respect that.

After checking in at the desk I followed him to the elevator. There was this older white couple standing behind us going up as we were. When the doors closed, Brandon reached around and grabbed and huge handful of my ass. I guess he didn't want to be all affectionate in the lobby but the doing it in front of two old people; now that was funny.

"Stop that. At least wait till we get to the room!"

I heard the old lady grunt with disgust. The old guy didn't bite his tongue at all.

"Ya'll need to be ashamed of yourselves! Two grown men touching each other. It's not natural!"

When they got off the elevator on the third floor, I shot Brandon a look. "Why did you do that in front of those old people?"

"I just wanted to get a rise out of them." He said laughing.

"Well instead of you getting a rise out of them you got one out of me."

Brandon's eyes ran over my entire body. I could see that he was just as turned on as I was.

When the elevator doors opened upon the sixth floor, both of us quickly found our room and were all over one another before the door could close behind us. Brandon and I had talked about this moment ever since he left to go home after he came up here with Tracy. We have been secretly falling for one another for the past few months. I see why Tracy loves him so much. He's caring, understanding, funny, and best of all, he's fine as hell. In my mind, I know just how I want this to go down. I'm lying on the bed butt naked and Brandon kneels between my legs and gives me the best blowjob of all time. I hurried up and got out of my clothes while he was in the restroom.

When he came out I was lying on the bed with a hard dick just for him. He took off his clothes and walked over to the bed. I closed my eyes anticipating feeling his warm lips wrap around my dick. To my surprise he straddled my face and was pushing his ten-inch dick in my mouth. At first I was shocked but the taste of his salty dick was intoxicating. My mouth opened and I took as much of him in as possible. He fucked my face like it was a pussy. I even gagged a few times; he was stroking my face so good. I jacked my dick as he face fucked me. He even tea bagged me. He stood over me and lowered his giant balls into my mouth over and over kinda like you dunk tea bags into hot water. I feel wonderful being with him.

It was my turn to enjoy his beautiful luscious lips. I slid out from underneath him. He was standing on the bed. I jump on the bed in front of him and pushed him to his knees. He opened his mouth and sucked all of me in. When I looked down all I saw was his face up against my pelvis. He licked the entire length of my dick. Brandon's tongue followed the veins in my dick like a road map. I watched him as he stroked his dick while he sucked mine.

I got down off the bed and reached for my over night bag that had my Astroglide in it. I laid him back on the bed, took two fingers full of the gel and rubbed it against his anus. I pressed my fingers in to make sure he was well lubed.

Brandon's cell phone rang. The phone was on the nightstand. He looked at the caller I.D.

"You know this is Tracy right?" He said as I fingered his ass.

"Do you plan on answering it?"

"Hell nah!"

We let the phone ring as we continued our business. I couldn't help but think that my friend is home wondering if her man is cheating on her, and I'm here with my dick ready to go in his ass.

I slowly pressed my dick into Brandon. He obviously was not new to this.

"Go ahead and fuck me. I'm open."

That was all I needed to hear. I began to pound him. My balls slapped against his ass as I drilled him for all I was worth. He stroked his dick as I fucked him. We kissed like old lovers. The moment is beautiful. After a few minuets in that position Brandon looked at me and said, "I want to fuck you now"

Since he was already lying down I straddled him in the cowgirl position. I bounced up and down on his dick the same way several women have bounced on mine. He stroked me as I rode him. Several minutes into our lovemaking I was ready to cum. I shot my load on his chest as I sat on his dick. Brandon rubbed my offering into his skin as I continued to bounce. When it was his turn to cum I got off of him and wrapped my lips around his very erect dick. He shot load after load into my waiting mouth. I tried not to let one-drop hit the ground.

We lay next to each other in the bed in a sweaty heap. It felt good to lie next to a real man and not some guy trying to figure out if he's gay, bi, or straight. I rolled over on top of Brandon and asked "So what are we gonna do for the rest of the weekend?"

"What do you mean?"

"I mean I know that tomorrow you'll be with Tracy and you know we are all going to the club tomorrow night."

"Yeah, she mentioned something about that the other day. I guess I'll just have to admire you from afar."

This is going to be a real uncomfortable situation tomorrow night at the club. I want to spend more time with Brandon but I have to share him in order to not hurt my friend.

CHAPTER 12

Tracy

Saturday morning and I am supposed to be extremely happy but I'm not. Brandon is coming in town today. Lately I don't know if he's been acting strange or if I've let Michelle get to me. I stood in the bathroom mirror looking at myself and said, "I'm not going to let anything ruin my time with him today. I'm not going to argue about anything with him since I have such a small amount of time with him this weekend. He's leaving tomorrow and I want everything to be perfect. My cell phone rang.

"Hello?"

"Hey baby it's me."

"Brandon, how are you this morning?" I tried to sound as cheerful as possible

"I'm good. I should be at your house in a couple of hours."

"Good. I put the good sheets on the bed this morning." I said in a very seductive voice.

"Oh I'm staying at the Ramada on Arlington."

I wanted to scream in the phone Why the fuck are you staying in a hotel when I have a house in town. But I held my tongue and went along with it. Something's not right. It just does not make sense to me to pay for a hotel when your girlfriend has a house. Walked into the front room, Michelle was sitting on the sofa eating a bowl of grits and eggs. I needed someone to talk to and since she was the only person at the house I figured, what the hell, she'll have to do.

"Michelle, let me ask you something."

She sat straight up and looked as if she was paying close attention.

"Brandon is staying in a hotel this weekend, instead of here with me."

Before I could get another word out she jumped right in. "Some funny shit is going on! Don't no nigga pay for a room unless he has to!"

I didn't want to admit it but Michelle and I were actually on the same page.

"What do you think I should do?"

"That's between you and your man. I'm staying out of that."

It felt like my feet were on fire and the flames were moving up my spine.

"What the fuck you mean, you staying out of it. You the one got me thinking he's doing something. When I come to you as a friend you turn your back on me! That's fucked up!"

"I just got you to start thinking. That's all I did. If your man is doing some dirt, then that's on you. Maybe your game ain't tight enough to keep him at home."

I was ready to knock the hell out of her for saying that to me. She started all of this, now she's dumping it on me. My eyes swelled up with water. I was so angry, I was ready to cry. The last thing I wanted to do was hear anymore she had to say, but that didn't stop her mouth from running.

"Look Tracy, I'm sorry. I should have been a little more sensitive to your needs than I was, and I apologize."

All I can do is smile. Every time I'm ready to jump on her ass she turns around and acts like she has some damn sense.

"No problem. It's just that he's been acting weird and I want to know why. If it's somebody else all he has to do is tell me and we can work it out."

"He's only here for a day and a half. Fuck the hell out your man and let his ass go back to Miami. Worry about that other shit later. Tonight is gonna be a lot of fun, so don't mess it up with a lot of drama. If he's doing something, it's sure to come out anyway."

About twenty minutes later, Eric walked in the house. He is smiling from ear to ear. Michelle started with her questions

"So where's your boy B?"

"He said he's going to meet me at the club tonight. He's gone to hang out with some cousins he has that stay up here."

I couldn't help but be nosey myself.

"What did ya'll do last night?" As if I didn't know.

"We fucked like two long lost lovers. I would go into detail but I don't want ya'll heifers to steal any of my signature moves. But I will tell you this after we were done we lay in bed and just held each other. It was a beautiful moment."

I long for the day when Brandon is able to hold me like that again. I'm going to take Michelle's advice and fuck his brains out tonight after we get back from the club. All of a sudden I felt excited to see him. It seemed like all my concerns flew out the window.

I heard my cell phone start ringing in my room. I ran in and without looking at the caller I.D. I answered the phone.

"Hey baby!" Thinking I was talking to Brandon

"Now that's the way I like you to answer the phone."

I instantly wanted to vomit. It was Byron. His voice just makes me want to throw up.

"What do you want? I have a busy day ahead of me."

"I just wanted to say thank you for a wonderful dinner."

"Good, great. I'm glad one of us had a good time. But look, I have to go. Like I said, I'm busy today. All day!"

"Go handle your business. I'll catch up with you later"

"Much later!"I hung up the phone. I turned around and Michelle was standing at my bedroom door.

"Damn I would hate to be the person you were just talking to."

I didn't realize she had heard me talking to Byron. "Girl that was one of those customer service people calling 'bout some bull they're selling."

"Yeah okay."

She turned and walked away. I really hope she didn't hear my entire conversation with Byron. Just like that, all the happiness I was starting to feel for Brandon was sucked away by Byron. Trying to stay focused on my man is a hard task when the person I hate is in the picture. I had to do something to get myself back in the right frame of mind.   I packed an overnight bag just in case I ended the evening in the hotel with my man. I put all the necessities in it. A thong, outfit for the next day, hair curler and my toothbrush.

I heard a car pull up in the front of the house. I looked through my bedroom window and saw Brandon step out of his car. My heart started to race. I couldn't get out of my room fast enough to go greet him at the door. Eric was standing at the door ready to open it when I jumped in the way.

"Let me open the door for my man please!" I said in a sarcastic voice.

"Go head then!"

He sucked his teeth and walked away. I thought what was that about. But as soon as I opened the door all my attention, love, and focus was on Brandon. I wrapped my arms around his neck. The smell of his cologne, Allure, was in the air. I felt his large hands rub my lower back. It felt great to have my man back with me. Michelle and Eric just stood back and let me have my moment. I hadn't paid any attention to what Michelle was wearing until I saw her walking towards Brandon to say hello. She's wearing skin tight jeans and a too small wife beater, with a red lace bra on underneath. Her eyes roamed all over his body as she stood in front of him trying to act like he wouldn't notice her big titties shaking from side to side in his face. That was grounds for an ass beating for disrespecting me like that, but I held my tongue with her again. Eric walked up to Brandon and shook his hand. Eric didn't really say much to Brandon; they just kinda looked at each other and walked away.

Brandon and I walked into my room. Lying on the bed, I hoped that Brandon would see me and instantly want to make love to me.

"Baby come lay down next to me you must be tired from the long drive."

He walked over to the bed and lay next to me. I slid my hand under his shirt and felt his well shaped chest. He began to rub my breast. My nipples instantly jumped hard. I rolled over on top of him and we kissed like we had not seen each other for five years. His dick was hard enough to cut a diamond and it had been a long time since we were last together and I need to feel him in me. I stood up to take off my pants when I heard another car pull into the driveway. While I was standing there, I looked out the window. I saw a girl from school walking up to the door.

Brandon asked, "Who's out there?"

"Some girl, I guess, for Eric"

I continued to take my clothes off. Brandon looked as if he was struggling to hear something. I heard Eric and the girl from outside talking and they sounded like they were walking towards his room. "I thought he was bi, but every time I see him he's with a girl."

"Eric is bi. He likes dick too," I said laughing. Thing is, I'm the only one who was laughing. I walked over to Brandon wearing nothing at all. I even shaved my pubic hair totally off to add a little newness and excitement to it. But, for some reason he seemed like he was preoccupied with something else. Through the walls I heard R. Kelly's 12 play come on.

"What the fuck is that!" Brandon asked with an irritated voice.

"I guess Eric is about to get some. He always turns the music up when he's about to handle his business. Now can we handle ours?" I was trying not to get pissed off but, when your girl is standing in front of you butt naked, and you are asking questions about somebody else that is getting some, we have a problem. Dropping to my knees I knew Brandon loved getting head. I licked his balls as he lay stiff on the bed. I took him in my mouth and slobbered all over it. As I pulled my lips away, a long string of spit hung from my lips to his dick. I sucked the spit back into my mouth like spaghetti. Brandon always loved to watch me suck him off. Finally he seemed like he was starting to get into it. Suddenly my cell phone rang. I had no intention of answering it and from the look on Brandon's face I don't think he heard it ring. It stopped ringing and I was still sucking him. The phone rang again. This time Brandon heard it and reached for it. I don't think he was going to answer it but I guess he wanted to see the caller I.D.

"No, no. Don't touch it!" I think I scared him the way I jumped up and started yelling.

"Damn aiight, I wasn't gonna answer it!"

Just like that, the mood was lost. Brandon was looking at me as if to say I'm hiding something or there is somebody on my phone I don't want him to know about. He listened to Eric and that girl go at it in the next room. I was more turned on by listening to them than actually having sex myself. The entire situation was weird, the louder Eric and his friend got, the madder Brandon became.

I bent down to pick up my clothes and looked at my phone that was on the nightstand next to my bed. The caller I.D. had Byron's number on it. I snatched it off the stand while I put on my panties and while Brandon had his back turned looking for his pants. If he ever found out that Byron was up here it would be over between us in the blink of an eye. Brandon has said in the past that he forgives me for what I did but if he found out about Byron now, I hate to even think about it.

For the rest of the afternoon, there was tension in the house. Brandon was not talking to Eric, and my phone rang so much that I just turned it off to not add to the tension. Not to mention, I was still a little upset with the way Michelle bounced around the house in front of Brandon. She even went so far as to leave the bathroom door unlocked when she was in there taking a shower this afternoon. Brandon didn't hear the water running and walked right in on her as she was bending over turning the water off. He looked right up her lumpy wet ass.

That night we all decided to go to Club Dynasty over on Green Street. Everybody in town goes to that club. The rest of the clubs were old redneck bars that none of us wanted to go to. We were about to leave for the club when Michelle asked Eric, "Where is B?"

"Oh, I talked to him earlier and he said he would meet us there."

"Is your girl Skye going? Or has she had enough of you for one day," she said laughing.

"Nah, I don't think she'll be there tonight"

Brandon looked at me and asked, "What kind of nigga fucks a girl named Skye. Sound like some hippie bitch."

I mumbled under my breath, "What kind of nigga passes up good pussy laying next to him?"

"You said something," Brandon asked?

"Huh? No I didn't say anything honey."

On the way to the club Brandon and I rode together, and Michelle and Eric rode together. Brandon hardly said a word to me the entire time in the car.

"What's wrong baby? You act like something's bothering you?"

"Nothing I'm cool."

We pulled up to the club and you could hear the music clear into the parking lot. They had Ushers song "Yeah" bumping inside. Once inside, the vibe in the club was hot. Everybody was looking good and feeling good. I must admit the ladies are representing tonight. If the club held five hundred people it was four hundred ninety nine in here. We found a table and I asked Brandon to go get me a drink. He quickly disappeared in the crowded club. The only other person at the table with me was Michelle and she was looking like a hawk looking for dinner. Every guy that walked by she tried to grab him or try to get him to buy her a drink. It was funny just sitting there watching the ghetto in action. This white guy walked up and Michelle flung her arms around him.

"Tracy, this is my boy Steve. Steve this is my roommate Tracy."

"Nice to meet you Steve."

He shook my hand then led Michelle to the dance floor. They were all over each other. I looked over to the bar and saw Brandon and Eric standing next to each other. It's good to see them actually having a conversation; even though Brandon does not look too happy to be standing there talking. As a matter of fact, he just walked away from Eric all together still standing at the bar.

Brandon walked back over to me and sat down. Michelle walked up and sat next to Brandon. She had on the shortest skirt in the club. All I could see was big thighs everywhere. Her breast looked like two brown bowling balls on her chest and she was getting a lot of attention because of them. A few hours into the club, Michelle had been doing a lot of drinking. She leaned over to Brandon. She thought she was whispering. "Would you like to dance with me?"

I'm not gonna sit here and be disrespected like that to my face.

"What the fuck is your problem!"

"What, what are you talking about?"

"Don't play with me bitch. I heard you ask my man to dance!"

Brandon stood up and grabbed Michelle's hand. He leaned down to me. "Baby look, don't start a scene in here. I'll dance one song with her drunk ass and that will be that."

She stared at me as she walked on the floor with my man. I looked around and saw Eric dancing with that girl I saw him with the first night I moved into the house. I thought, where is this B character he was happy about? But he's over there dancing with some hoochie. Nigga's ain't shit.

I looked back on the floor and saw Michelle all over Brandon. The song Move Your Body was on and she was following every word. I wanted to run out there and snatch her bald right on the floor. But I had to remember I'm a lady dealing with a hood rat. 112's "Crazy Over You" came on the system and everybody slowed down and grabbed a person to dance with. Michelle pulled Brandon close but I wasn't having any of that. Walking to the floor I saw another nerdy looking guy tap Brandon on the shoulder. Michelle looked like she wanted to faint. Brandon backed away and the nerdy guy started dancing with Michelle. The look on her face made the entire night better. She looked like she wanted to fall through the ground. She was so embarrassed.

On the way home from the club Brandon and I stopped to get a bite to eat at the Waffle House. The parking lot was packed with everybody from the club. I spotted Michelle in the car with that white guy Steve. I guess she ditched the nerd. Brandon looked at me.

"Do you want to eat here?"

"This is fine."

"Cool I'll go in and see how long the wait for a table will be."

As soon as Brandon walked away from the car, another car rolled up next to me. The window rolled down and it was Byron. My heart fell to my feet. Brandon was no more than fifty feet away from us.

"What the fuck are you doing here!"

"It's a free country I can go where the fuck I please!"

"Look, you have to leave!"

"Why 'cause your boy is here? I don't think so!"

"Please don't do this to me. If you love me as much as you say you do then please don't do this to me. Not tonight."

He looked me dead in my eyes and made me a promise "I'm going to have you Tracy. You can bank on that!" Brandon was walking back to the car when Byron rolled up his window and drove off.

"Who was that?" Brandon asked as he got back in the car.

"It was some dude asking for directions to another club"

I looked around the parking lot and happened to look right in Michelle's face staring at me.

"On second thought baby, let's go some place else." I said, just to get out of that parking lot.

How did Byron know where I was? How did he know what car I was in? This shit is starting to get crazy.

CHAPTER 13

Michelle

8/8/04

That bitch had the nerve to roll up the window in my face. It's not my fault she damn near got busted talking to her ex. Well, actually it is my fault. Ever since I found out about her and Byron I've made it my business to keep him aware of everything she does. Including going to the club with her man. I guess that's the ghetto coming out of me. I took her situation and made it work for Byron and I. I enrolled in his class and told him I knew about him and Tracy. And if I didn't pass his class with flying colors and keep my scholarship I would go to the Dean and tell everything I know. Byron was more than willing to go along with me on this as long as I kept him informed of what Tracy was doing and who she was seeing. Sounds like a win, win situation to me. Well at least for Byron and me.

I closed my journal and couldn't help laughing a little to myself. Tracy looked as if she had seen a ghost when she looked in my face at the restaurant. I walked from my bedroom to the family room and saw Brandon coming out of the bathroom. He is so fine I thought, as I walked up behind him.

"Can I help you with your bags Brandon?" I said in my fuck me voice. He turned and looked at me. My breasts were in his eye line and he didn't try to hide the fact that he was looking right at them.

"Nah I'm cool."

I knew that if I had half a second alone with him, I'd fuck his brains out. I don't see what men see in those skinny ass women anyway. Most of the men I've fucked say they like a woman with a little meat on her bones because when they are hitting the pussy on a big girl it feels good to them. But, on a skinny girl their pelvis is hitting her pelvis and they say that shit don't feel good at all. I guess with my titties staring at him his dick got a little excited and started trying to make an appearance. He quickly turned around and started walking back toward Tracy's room for the rest of his things. I peeked in the room behind him and saw that Tracy was still asleep. I figured why not go for it.

"Brandon?"

He walked right at me and stopped just short of bumping into me. "Wuz up?"

"Let's sit on the sofa and talk for a minute"

He placed another bag by the door and motioned me to the sofa. Walking over, I made sure to add a little more wiggle to my walk. He was behind me and I could feel his eyes all over my ass. He sat with his back to Tracy bedroom door which was good for me so I could see her if she walked out of her room. I started the conversation. "I'm gonna be straight forward. What do you see in ya girl?"

At first he looked at me like I had lost my mind, then he gave me an unexpected answer. "Well, I'm with her cause I know with her I'll never have to worry about money or be in any bad financial situations."

My mouth just fell open. I didn't know what to say in response to that. He continued. "That girl's family takes good care of her. She don't have to work unless she wants to. The only reason she's in college is because her parents told her she had to get a degree or they were going to cut her off and she was going to have to make it on her own. Her grandpa loves me so much, for a wedding gift he has bought us a million dollar mansion, fully furnished, and a trust fund with enough money in it to live another hundred years without having to work. It's all ready for us after we get married.

"So you put up with her being snotty all the time, being hateful to everybody, and worst of all, cheating on you before?"

He sat back on the sofa and took a deep breath then answered. "I put up with her 'cause I'm not stupid. See, what you don't understand is that my father is a preacher of a small church back home. It pays the bills and we do okay. But her family comes from a long line of money. Those people are still spending her great grandfather's money. They haven't touched her grandpa or their money yet."

I was still shocked. I thought this boy is worse than I am. He's using Tracy to get the money. Damn, I love a dirty ass nigga.

He looked over his shoulder to make sure Tracy was not moving around in her room and moved a little closer to me. He leaned over and whispered in my ear, "I love a thick woman anyway. Tracy told me that the two you didn't get along, but since the last time I saw you, I can't seem to get you off my mind. If I could have her money and your heart, I'd be the happiest man on earth.

With those words I think I just came on myself. I could tell by the way he looked at me he was serious. Hell, I'd even be his mistress if he wanted me to be.. He reached up and grabbed my breasts. My nipples got hard almost instantly. He gently pinched my nipples through my shirt. I could feel the wetness starting to run down my thighs. I lay back on the sofa and opened my legs offering him a clear view of my black thong. Brandon eyes lit up like a Christmas tree. He leaned forward and with his right hand and gently massaged my wet vagina through my panties. I closed my eyes and relaxed as Brandon fingers worked their magic. I heard Brandon's voice. "If I had known you were this big a freak, I would have tried to hit this that first night at the party."

"You should have just come in the bathroom and handled your business." I felt Brandon's hands moving up towards my hips. He grabbed my panties and was working them down under my butt. I raised off the sofa a little to make sure he could get them off without a problem. I looked over his shoulder to make sure Tracy was still asleep. I didn't see any movement so I let him continue. Eric wasn't home so we didn't have to worry about him walking in on us. I watched as Brandon licked his lips and spread my thighs ever further apart. I sat back and closed my eyes knowing that the next thing I felt would be Brandon's tongue lapping at my very wet pussy. His breath felt good warming my inner thighs as he moved in to taste me. He spread my lips apart and then there was a knock at the door. My eyes popped open.

"What the fuck! Who the fuck is that?" I asked. Looking over Brandon's shoulders I could see that the knock at the door had woke Tracy up and she was beginning to stir around in her bed. The person at the door knocked again. This time I heard Tracy shuffling her feet looking for her bedroom slippers. As I jumped from the sofa Brandon shoved my panties in his pocket. I went to the door with the biggest attitude under the sun, Snatching the door open "Who is it!"

Standing in front of me was Prentice, looking like a lost puppy.

"What man! What the fuck do you want?"

"I saw you at the club all over some dude last night!"

"So and?"

"I thought you and I were supposed to be together. I don't appreciate you being all over somebody else."

Right then, hell was about to break loose. "I know you're not standing on my porch, trying to talk shit to me. Muthafucka I told you last time, I would fuck you up if you ever tried to punk me again! I got half a mind to go grab some hot grits and toss 'em on your punk ass!"

He surprised me and stood his ground. I was expecting him to fold up like a sheet of paper after I screamed at him.

"My boys told me you were a hood rat and I was way too good for a bitch like you. But did I listen...? No. I'm looking like a damn fool taking you to lunch and driving you around!"

I wanted to grab him and choke the hell out of him. Without even thinking I punched him in him jaw. I braced myself for a rumble but it never happened. Prentice just stood there.

"That's all right. I'll fix your ass. Trust that," he said as he walked off the porch.

I slammed the door and turned around to see Tracy and Brandon both standing there watching the entire scene unfold. Tracy started in on me first.

"That was the nerdy guy I was telling you about at the club. He came to our house?"

"Yeah, that's Prentice he's this young cat I met, used him for a few dollars, now he think he owns me."

Brandon jumped in. "He should have kicked your ass for punching him. My mama always told me, if a woman is man enough to hit you, then she's man enough to get her ass whipped."

Sucking my teeth, I walked past Brandon who had my panties balled up in his hands and put them in my hand as I walked by. Tracy didn't see any of this 'cause she was standing on the other side of him as I walked by. I looked back and saw him rubbing her hair with the same hand he had my panties in. I walked in my room closed the door and burst out laughing.

Later that afternoon, I heard Brandon say his good bye's and got in his car. I picked up the phone and called Byron.

"Hello?"

"Byron this is Michelle. I just want you to know that her boyfriend just left."

"Did he? So I guess I can come around there now huh?"

"Yeah, but check this out. I need you to try and fuck her in the front room."

"Why?"

" Just try to hit it in the front room, that's all."

In a very cocky voice he said, "You want to watch don't you?"

"Hell no. I just need you to try and do that for me."

After hanging up the phone, I heard the shower start running. Tracy was taking her afternoon shower. That bitch took more showers than anybody I know. I took this opportunity to get a little insurance for myself. I figured since Brandon was getting paid, I might as well get my share of the pie as well. I took my hand held video camera and set it up between some books on a shelf in the front room. The camera was hard to see if you were not looking for it. As I was finishing up hiding the recorder, I heard Eric's keys hit the door. I turned the television on and sat on the sofa as he entered the house.

"Wuz up girl?" He said sounding tired and worn out.

"Wuz up with you?"

"I just left my girl Skye house. That girl love to fuck. Damn

I had to beg her to let me get some sleep. I don't want to do shit but go to sleep."

This was working out perfectly. I needed some place to go and he's right on time, to take me out the house before Byron got here.

"Eric before you go to sleep can you run me to the mall right quick?"

"What! Come on man. I just got home!"

"Please, I need to go pick something up. It will only take a few minutes."

"Fine, give me ten minuets and we can go."

"Thank you, you know you my nigga right?"

"Just when we get there, hurry up and get what you are gonna get so I can get back home!"

I went back in the room to get dressed. I called Byron and told him to be to the house in about 15 minuets. He agreed.

As Eric and I were getting ready to walk out the door Tracy walked out of her room. She's wearing a pair of cut off jeans and a wife beater. I thought Byron is gonna love to see her in that. As we walked out the door I asked Eric, "So I guess your boy B stood you up at the club huh?"

He looked at me like I was not minding my business then answered, "Nah, he was there but he was trippin' about something. That's why I was with Skye the rest of the night."

"Damn, you should have introduced us before you ditched the man!"

"I didn't ditch him. I just don't have time to waste on confused people."

We got in the car and headed towards the mall. About 10 blocks away from the house we saw Byron coming towards us.

"Ain't that Professor Caldwell over there?" Eric asked.

"That look like him, don't it?"

I knew damn well that was him and I knew where he was headed.

Eric added to the conversation "All I know is, that nigga's fine as hell. He gives me thirty seconds with his ass and I'll have him bent over calling me daddy."

CHAPTER 14

Eric

"Hello?"

"Brandon, this is Eric"

"I can't believe you!"

"What the hell is wrong with you? I thought we were going to have a great time while you were here but you tripped all day Saturday and just left Sunday without saying a word to me."

"Well if you didn't have that bitch over there Saturday, we could have had a great time!"

"You do know I still like women right?" I can't believe that he is trippin' on me because I was with a woman when he was there with his girlfriend.

"Yeah I know you like women, but you didn't have to flaunt it all in my face that you were going to be with one."

"Look, I'm not even gonna have this conversation with you. I like pussy and I like dick. Whichever one I want at the moment is what I'm gonna get. Okay, deal with it or leave me the fuck alone. But either way, this conversation is done." I hung up the phone, furious with Brandon for acting like a bitch. Walking into the front room to watch a little television Tracy was sitting on the sofa looking like she had lost her best friend.

"What's wrong boo?"

"It's Brandon. I think he's cheating on me."

I thought, your ass is always crying bout some shit. If I were your man I'd cheat on you too. But being the good friend that I am I asked, "You feel like talking about it?"

She wiped her eyes and began talking. "I just called him a little while ago and I guess he was on the phone with somebody.

He just said, let me call you back, and hung up the phone. He always makes time for me. Even if he's on the phone with his family, he always put me first. Something is wrong I'm losing my man."

"Girl that man loves you. I see the way he looks at you when ya'll are together. He stared at you the entire time we were in the club. Did you see him and me standing at the bar that night?"

"Yes."

"He was telling me how much he loves you and how you are his world." Sometimes I lie so well I surprise myself. But my friend needs me right now. I'll tell her anything she wants to hear if I think it will make her feel better. That's what true friends do.

"I know he loves me, he has put up with so much. I want to be the woman he wants me to be but lately he's been very distant with me."

"Maybe he's going through a little something right now. Give him a little time and I bet he'll start acting right." I could say that because I knew if he tripped on me again, he wouldn't have to worry about me ever again.

Later that night Michelle and I decided to go grab a bite to eat. On the way to China Buffet, our favorite Chinese restaurant, Michelle started a conversation that would change the way I looked at her and everyone involved.

"Eric, I have to tell you something that's gonna trip you out."

I turned down the radio and listened to what she had to say.

"Your girl Tracy ain't shit"

"Why you say that?"

"'Cause she's fucking a teacher"

I almost lost control of the car. I pulled over into the next parking lot we came to and put the car in park.

"What did you say?"She was going to have to repeat that. I had to make sure I heard her correctly.

"She's fucking one of her teachers"

"Which one?"

"See, I can't tell you all that, but I do know that she's been doing it for a while now."

"See, why you playin'? Tell me who the teacher is!" I had to know. I do remember reading something in her journal that said she was with a guy named Byron. But that was way back in Miami.

"Wait a second Michelle. Why should I believe you? You ain't never liked Tracy."

"Me liking her ain't got shit to do with what I'm telling you. I just thought you might want to know your housemate was fucking Byron Caldwell. Damn, did I say his name? My bad."

I sat in my seat, motionless. I could not believe what I was hearing. The Byron she wrote about was her teacher. And, now they are up here together. This time with no Brandon to get in the way.

"Michelle, how did you find all this out."

"It's all in her journal. I was in her room one day looking for a hair clip and ran across it lying open on her bed and the name Byron caught my eye and I found out more than what I wanted to."

I knew she wasn't lying about stuff like that being in her journal. I do question whether it was lying open on the bed or not, but that's not the case. The case is now I can have my man all to myself.

Once inside the restaurant, I excused myself to go to the rest room. I went into one of the stalls and made a phone call.

"Hello?"

"Brandon you are not going to believe this," I said whispering into the phone.

"What do you want Eric?"

"Listen, I just found out that Tracy is fucking one of her teachers."

"First off, don't call me with your lies and secondly why are you whispering."

"'Cause I'm in a restaurant restroom, and does the name Byron Caldwell ring a bell?"

He went silent for a second. His breathing became loud and fast.

"Yeah, that was one of her teachers when she was down

here."

"Well, he's up here now and she's still sleeping him."

"How do you know?"

"I have my sources."

"Well tell your sources to mind their business."

I didn't know what to think. This is not the reaction I had hoped for. I just knew that he would be yelling and cursing and damning her name. But it's like he could care less. Since he didn't get angry at her, now I'm pissed with him. "What the fuck is wrong with you! You got pissed off because I was with a woman while you were here, and now I tell you that your girl is still cheating on you and you act like it doesn't bother you one bit. This is a chance for us to be together and you are letting it go right out the window!"

"Let me be honest with you. I like sleeping with you, don't get me wrong. And, I actually care about you, but I don't want to be with you like that. I don't want to spend the rest of my life with you."

My heart felt like it stopped for a few seconds. I got instantly dizzy. I just hung up the phone and sat on the toilet for a while. His words sent me over the edge. How could he not want me? Our chemistry is wonderful. Or at least I thought it was. My eyes filled with tears. I wanted to breakdown and cry.

Once I got myself together I walked back into the dinning area. Michelle had a plate of fried shrimp, pork fried rice, chicken wings, and those sugar-coated fried dumplings. I went through the line and came back with a bowl of Won Ton Soup. I was not in the mood for eating. I had lost my man and my appetite.

As I sat sipping at my soup I saw Skye and a few of her friends walk into the restaurant. At first she didn't realize I was there. All I could do was hope that the waiter didn't walk her past our table. I would have no such luck. As her friends walked past our table Skye stopped.

"So, I guess I'm spoiling your little date huh!"

I was not in the mood for some funny shit. "Skye you know this is my roommate Michelle."

"I can see that but what I don't understand is why ya'll all out up under each other!"

Almost every head in the place was now looking in our direction.

"Skye ain't shit going on here. We are just out grabbing a bite to eat."

That's when all hell broke loose. "Hold up Eric, you don't have to explain shit to this trick!" Michelle stood up and was in Skye's face.

Skye was much smaller than Michelle. Skye's crew didn't even come over to back her up. They just walked off. As she realized she had just got punked she turned and looked towards me.

"This ain't over Eric. And Michelle, watch your back!"

"Fuck you bitch. Go sit down," Michelle yelled, as Skye went to the other side of the restaurant.

"Come on Michelle, let's go."

"Why we got to leave? I haven't got my second plate yet."

"Girl, I'll treat you to some Burger King. Let's get the hell out of here."

We left before any other altercations could happen. In the car Michelle started with all the questions again. "What's up with you and Thomas?"

"He ain't trying to get down with a brother. I tried to edge him in my direction but he's sold on some pussy so I just gave up the chase. We're still cool but it will have to be a determined effort on my part and I ain't trying to devote an entire year trying to fuck one guy.

CHAPTER 15

Tracy

My world is upside down. My man is tripping and I can't get away from my past. I hate having to come to his class. As I walk down the hall way I get to his class door. I hear a familiar voice.

"Why would I have to lie?"

"Fine, I believe you, just keep me posted."

I walked into the room and saw Michelle and Byron talking. My eyes almost fell out of my head. They both looked as if they had seen a ghost. Byron walked over to me and tried to explain. "Hey Tracy. How's it going? Michelle and I were just talking about her trying to get into the culinary program."

Michelle chimed in on time. "Well Professor Caldwell, I'll be sure to get back to you about that okay?"

"Yes Michelle, you have a great day."

I guess they thought I was stupid. I knew something was up but I didn't know what. I walked over to Byron. "I want to end this between us Byron. It's causing me to lose people that I really care for."

"Okay then. Not a problem. You want it over, it's over."

I was shocked. He seemed to be serious. He went back to writing in his book, without even looking back at me.

"I'm glad we were able to handle this like adults."

"Yeah me too. Well look, I have to make a stop at the post office to mail that tape of us together to your parents before my next class. So if you'll excuse me."

He tried to walk past me but I jumped in his way.

"But, I thought you said it was cool if we ended this?"

"Oh it is cool, but if we end this I'm going to have to mail that package. See, what you don't seem to understand is that I say when it's over between us. Not you."

If looks could kill he'd been dead soon after those words fell from his lips.

"I fucking hate you!"

"So, and?"

I just walked towards the door. His words stopped me before I could walk out.

"So I guess tonight is a good night for us to get together then. I like it when you're all pissed off. The pussy is great when you're mad. I'll give you a call later tonight."

I stormed out of the classroom. I could no longer take being with Byron. I am going to take matters into my own hands.

I walked across campus with a purpose. I didn't stop to talk to anybody. I was on a mission. I walked into the Add and Drop Department and withdrew from Byron's class. When he calls me tonight, yes, I'm going to meet him and tell him exactly what I think about him and his little tape he's holding over my head. I walked out of that office feeling liberated. I know that I'm taking a huge risk by doing this, but I have to end this.

On the way home from campus, I called Brandon's cell phone. He had gone back to Miami and I had not spoken to him in a few days.

"Hello?"

"Hey baby, it's me."

"Hold on, let me turn my music down…okay, Tracy, how are you doing today?"

"I'm good. Look, I just want to tell you how much I really love you."

"I love you too baby, you know that."

"I know, but I just need to hear that from you every so often. But look. There might be something coming to your house. I don't know what it will contain, but just remember that I love you."

"You're sending me something?"

"You can say that."

When I hung up the phone I noticed that Brandon and I

were listening to the same song on the radio and it was at the same point in the song. That's really strange, or is that a sign that we are more connected than we thought. It's meant for us to be together. I walked in the house and went directly to my room. I picked out the most revealing dress I had and laid it across the bed. I said to myself I want that nigga to see what he'll never get again.

A few hours passed, and finally my cell phone rang.

"Hello?"

"I told you I was gonna call you."

"Yeah, I've been waiting"

"You have?"

"Yeah, I'm tired of fighting you. It's obvious that you love me and it's time I stop denying myself the one man that really cares for me."

The phone went silent. For the first time I felt in control of Byron.

"Well, meet me at my house in, say, in thirty minutes."

"I'll be there."

I hung up the phone and started to laugh a little. I knew that tonight I was gonna finally end it. This would be the last time I would have to see this man. As a matter of fact, I'm going to take out a restraining order tomorrow.

I walked into the front room. Michelle sat straight up when she looked at me in my dress.

"Damn, you need to let me rock that one night to the club!"

"I tell you what, after tonight, I'll let you have it." Then I mumbled to myself, not that your fat ass would ever get it on.

When I pulled up to Byron's house, I thought, this poor, sad muthafucka has no idea what's about to go down. I guess he was watching me walk up the walkway. He opened the door before I could ring the bell.

"Now, that's what I'm talking about. You look good tonight!" I had never seen him so giddy.

"Well thank you." I walked in the house and stood right next to the door. There was no way I was going to walk any further into the house. "Please, let's go into the den"

He stuck out his arm showing me the way.

"No, actually I have to tell you something." I backed up against the door. He couldn't tell but I had my hand on the doorknob just in case I had to make a run for it.

"What is it baby?" He looked concerned and attentive.

"It's over between us. I don't care if you send that tape to my parents. I don't care if you send it to Brandon 'cause he and I are no longer together anyway." I gripped the door handle, ready to run.

Byron just stood there staring at me. His face went from concern to pure hate. He lunged at me. "Come here bitch!"

I snatched open the door and ran like hell to my car. I fumbled with the keys, trying to press the remote to unlock the doors. I didn't know if he was behind me and I didn't turn around to see. I heard the doors unlock and I just jumped in my car locked the door and started the engine. When I finally looked up the front door was closed. I hit the gas as I backed out the driveway. I noticed one of his neighbors was outside watering his yard.

"I know that man must think I'm crazy as hell," I said to myself as I sped down the street.

My cell phone rang over and over. I looked at the caller I.D. and it was Byron. I drove around town for a little while, trying to calm myself down. My hands were shaking and my heart felt like it was about to jump out of my chest. I hadn't realized that I had been driving around for three hours. I went into a convenience store to grab a soda. The older white guy behind the counter tried to talk to me but I wasn't having it. I went home and went directly to Eric's room. He was standing in front of the mirror trying on some new clothes.

"Guess what?"

He turned around. "What?"

"I'm done."

"What are you talking about?"

I sat him on the bed and told him everything. I went all the way back to when I went to school in Miami. He sat and listened to me go on and on. He never interrupted me one time. I told him about the relationship between Byron and me. I told him about how mad Brandon was when he found out. I told him about the other night when I was over there. I told him everything. I guess you can say that I really trust Eric. After I told him everything, he pulled me close to him and held me tight. That's exactly what I needed at that point. A good hug.

The next morning I got up and felt wonderful. My cell phone had not ringed all night. The first thought I had, finally was not of Byron. I felt like a new woman. I went into the kitchen to have breakfast. Michelle sat to the table eating a bowl of cereal. I remembered I still needed to check her for the way she acted that night in the club with Brandon, but I even forgave her, I was feeling so good. I jumped in my car and headed for the campus. From a distance I saw emergency rescue lined up behind the culinary building. I drove up slow in traffic trying to get on campus. The school's security was directing traffic to go around where all the emergency vehicles were. I found a parking space on the other side of the campus. I heard several students talking as they were coming from the direction of the culinary buildings. I listened in on one conversation as they walked past me.

"They say his body has sat there for a while," one of the students said.

A body, I said to myself as I sped up a little to really find out what was going on. The front of the building was sealed off with yellow tape and police everywhere. I walked up to one of my professors and asked, "What happened?"

Her face was soaked with tears. "They found him dead this morning half in his car." Her voice was shaking after every word.

"Who's dead?"

"Professor Caldwell."

It was like everything was in slow motion. Everything went blank. I saw people moving but they were all in slow motion to me. I went to the parking lot. The police had it blocked off as well. I saw Byron's car and a black filled body bag was on the ground next to it. There was blood all over the place. The police were asking people if they saw anything, to come to them and tell what they knew. I turned to walk away and one of the detectives walked up to me.

"Hello miss, did you see anything here today?"

"No officer."

"You sure. Did you see or hear anything at all?"

"No sir. When I left him last night everything was fine." Right then I wanted to take back every word I had just said. As soon as those words fell from my lips I knew I was in way over my head.

"You were with him last night?"

I knew I couldn't lie, I would only look guilty. "Yes detective. I was over at his house last night."

"Do you mind going to the station and answering a few questions?"

"No sir. Anything I can do to help, I will."

Me and my big mouth. I went to the station and told them everything I knew about Byron. What happened next, I'll never forget for the rest of my life. They had me sitting in a small room. Two detectives asked me question after question about Byron. Finally one of them said, "Tracy we're going to let you go. But, don't leave town. We may need you back here for more questioning."

Even in his death he still has control of my life.

CHAPTER 16

Michelle

The campus was still in shock as the news of Byron's murder ran rampant. A student found his body in his car, is the story I'm being told. But the surprising part that has everybody talking is they saw Tracy getting in a police car at the scene. I found Eric sitting with Skye in the student union. Skye saw me before Eric did and her smile went south as I walked through the door.

"Hey Eric, you got a minute. We need to talk!"

Before Eric could say a word Skye jumped in. "No he don't have a minute, he's with me now. I take up all his minutes"

I had, had enough.

"Look bitch, I'm tired of your funky ass talking shit to me! Open your mouth again and I'm gonna fuck you up right here, right now. Now try me!"

She looked as if she was going to jump, bad But Eric stopped her from getting the beating of her life.

"Hey wuz up Michelle? Skye give us a minute."

She looked at him like he had just cursed out her mother. She hopped up and stomped off like a child.

"Eric, have you heard about Professor Caldwell?"

"Yeah, I heard they found him dead in his car."

"Yeah, but did they tell you who they took downtown in the police car?"

"No who?"

"Tracy."

He didn't move or blink. He just sat there I guess waiting on me to say I was just trippin'.

Finally he asked me, "Are you serious?"

"As a heart attack."

"I need to call Brandon and tell him what's going on."

"Yeah, that's a good idea. Tell him he needs to come up here."

This is going to work out in my favor. If she's locked up for killing Byron and Brandon is up here I'm going to fuck the hell out of him and there is nothing she could do about it. Life is good. I heard Eric on the phone talking to Brandon as I left the student union.

I had my white boyfriend, Steve, bring me home. As soon as he pulled off, an unmarked police car pulled up.

"May we talk to you ma'am?"

"Sure. What's on your mind officer?"

"We're trying to find out about your roommate Tracy."

"What about her?" Hell, I really didn't like that bitch anyway, so what ever they wanted to know I was going to tell them.

"Did she have a relationship with Byron Caldwell?"

"Yes she did. They were lovers."

The cop looked stunned for a second.

"So the two of them were in a romantic relationship?"

"Yes."

"Did they have an argument or anything like that, that you know of?"

"Well, towards the end of the relationship she was trying to break it off with him. I don't think he was taking it too well."

"That's all I'm going to need from you for now. I'll be in touch."

I went to my room and began cleaning up. There is nothing stopping me from fucking Brandon this time. He's a good man and deserves a woman like me. Eric walked into the house.

"Brandon should be here in a few hours. He said he would be on the first plane coming this way as soon as he gets to the airport." I need to head to the mall to get something special for this occasion.

"Eric, can I use your car to go to the mall real quick?"

"Yeah, in about an hour. I need to run to the library to pick up something."

"Okay, that's fine. Thanks." I am as giddy as a schoolgirl looking at her first crush. I can't wait to see him again. Hell, I'll even play female number two just to get some of Tracy's money and fuck her man. I'm in a win, win situation.

About an hour later Eric returned with the car. "Be careful with my ride!"

Eric loved his car more than he loved himself. That car was his all and all.

"Yeah Eric, no problem."

I headed to the mall as fast as I could. I knew the store I was going to and I was in the store the other day and saw the outfit I'm going to buy. I walked in the mall and headed right for Lane Bryant. Some people hate on big girls, but you know that it takes a real man to handle a sistah with a little meat on her bones. I picked up a pair of black lace thongs and a black lace Bra to match. I even went the extra mile and picked up stockings and a garter. If I was going to wow Brandon I was going all the way. Since Tracy was, nine times out of ten, locked up, I took the liberty of picking up a white outfit just in case Brandon stayed an extra day. I went over to Payless Shoe Store and picked up a pair of cheap black heels. It didn't make sense to go out and buy an expensive pair of shoes when they were just gonna be over my head and around his waist most of the time.

As I walked out of the shoe store I saw a man that looked just like Brandon. "Brandon!"

The guy kept walking. He had the same shape, haircut and even the same walk. I might be mistaken since the guy is about a good two hundred feet in front of me. I guess this town has more than one fine ass guy in it. I tried to catch up with the guy but he went into Dillard's, and by the time I got there he was nowhere to be found. I must admit, that had me baffled a little bit.

It had been a few hours since Eric told Brandon what was going on. I decided to go home and get things ready for my soon-to- be man. I drove up to the house and there was a car that I had not seen before parked in the driveway. It was a black Toyota Camry with Texas plates.

"Who the fuck is this over here now?" I asked myself as I

walked past the car. "Just what I need, somebody else in the house cock blocking." I opened the front door and familiar cologne hit me in the face. "Damn I know the smell," I said as I walked in the kitchen. I sat at the table and thought about my plans for when Brandon came back in town. My thoughts were interrupted by moaning sounds. "That nigga Eric must have one of his bitches over here." I tried to ignore it but the moans got louder and louder. Then I realized that the moans I was hearing were coming from two men. One moan was lower than the others. I knew Eric was bi so it didn't bother me that he was having sex with another man. From the sounds they were making, somebody was getting fucked real good. I went into the front room and turned the television on. I tried to tune them out, but they were really loud. I turned the volume up and I still heard them. Things really got outrageous when I heard Eric.

"You love this dick don't you?"

I started to giggle till I heard the second voice

"Hell yeah nigga, fuck this ass!"

For a second it seemed like everything stopped. The voice I heard was extremely familiar. Then I heard the second man's voice again. "My turn Eric. I've got to fuck your tight ass."

In my heart, I knew who it was but I didn't want to believe it. There was no way this could be happening. I got up and walked slowly to Eric's bedroom door. I see why I heard everything so clear; the door was not closed all the way. The closer I got to Eric's room the louder and clearer I heard them. My heart was pounding. I noticed my hands were starting to shake a little as I leaned closer to the door to look through the crack. My mouth fell open. I stopped breathing for a second when I saw Eric and Brandon's sweaty bodies all over one another.

I stood to the door and watched through the crack as Brandon pounded Eric's ass. Brandon fucked him the way I wanted him to fuck me. Eric was in the doggy style position. Brandon was behind him smacking him on the ass as he drilled him. Eric stroked his own dick as Brandon fucked him hard and fast. The two of them went at one another like two lost lovers.

"Let me ride you backwards baby?" Eric said as he let

Brandon's hard on slide out of his butt. The sight of two sexy men having sex was a major turn on for me. I felt my nipples start to harden under my shirt. I looked down at my chest to see how hard my nipples had gotten. When I looked up again Eric was staring me right in the face. I wanted to run but my feet wouldn't move. I wanted to say something but my voice was gone. Eric pulled the door wide open and I saw Brandon lying in the bed behind him.

Brandon's face looked like he had seen a ghost. He sat straight up in the bed and tried to explain.

"Michelle, before you get all crazy. I want you to know that I am a bi sexual man also."

I looked at him with a sarcastic smirk on my face. "Really? You don't say."

Eric jumped in. "Look, you know I love me a fine ass nigga and you must admit, Brandon is fine as hell. I couldn't live with myself knowing that I let him slip by without getting me a little taste."

I stood there, mind racing. "I'll be right back"

I ran to the kitchen grabbed my bags and went into my room. Before the door was closed I was half way out of my clothes. I grabbed a few baby wipes to freshen my cat a little and through on the white outfit I just purchased from Lane Bryant. I walked back to Eric's room. I pushed the door open and Eric was on his knees giving Brandon a blowjob.

"Mind if I join in the fun?" I said as I stood in the doorway looking, if I say so myself, sexy as hell. Both men looked up and their mouths dropped open.

"Hell yeah you can join in." Brandon said as he sat on the edge of the bed with his dick shinning with Eric's spit. Eric looked at me with a funny look on his face. I guess both of us never thought we would end up in this situation. But, just the thought of it was turning me on more and more by the second.

I walked over to the bed and rubbed on Brandon's muscular chest. He reached up and grabbed two handfuls of my breasts. Then I felt Eric's hand start to rub my butt. I was ready to cum on the spot. Both men were all over me. It felt like one hundred hands were touching me at the same time. I turned my head to the left and Eric had moved to that side. He stood in front of me with his dick in his hand. I opened my mouth and sucked him in as far as I could. I took long slow sucks on his hard dick. I motioned for Brandon to let me taste his dick. He walked over and I let Eric's dick fall out and I turned my head and started sucking Brandon. I was so into it I grabbed both their dicks and tried to stuff them both into my mouth at the same time. I only managed to get both heads in because they both have very large dicks.

Eric squeezed my breasts as I sucked him and Brandon off. I lay back on the bed and Brandon knelt down over my face and I finished sucking him off. I felt Eric go between my legs. Before I knew it, my legs were up in the air and I felt a tongue inside of me. Eric's tongue touched spots I didn't know I had. He gently nibbled on my clit while fingering me at the same time. I came all over Eric's face. He made me cum multiple times. I sucked on Brandon's balls as Eric's tongue found my G-spot over and over. I was in paradise. I rolled over on my side and threw my leg high in the air. I was ready for one of them to fuck me. Brandon was the first one up for the task. He lay behind me and I soon felt his huge dick stat nudging at my pussy. I gasped for air as he pushed his way into me. As Brandon started his steady rhythm, Eric walked over and shoved his dick back into my mouth. I could hardly contain myself. I had both men on me. Life was good. And it was to only get better.

CHAPTER 17

Eric

I had never considered myself attracted to Michelle, but I could not let this opportunity slip away. Over the years, our conversations have always been about sex for the most part. She's told me several things she'd done and I have always been a little intrigued by her stories, but now I get to witness her first hand.

I watched as Brandon fucked her while she lay on her side. A part of me was a little jealous at first, but then I saw the beauty of three people fucking at the same time, and I just wanted to be apart of that. "Brandon it's my turn to get a little of that pussy," I said as I pushed Brandon out the way. "Get on your knees and let me hit this doggy style."

Michelle was more than happy to oblige. She reached back and spread her butt cheeks as I had the perfect angle to dive right into her. I got behind her and Brandon had already had her wide open I just slid right in. I watched as her big butt cheeks wiggled every time I pushed into her. Brandon walked over and offered his dick for me to suck. Without even thinking about it I opened up my mouth and he shoved his dick in my face. I sucked him off as I fucked Michelle. Michelle watched me over her shoulder as I gave Brandon head. I slapped her on the ass the more excited I got. Before long, we all were talking to each other while we all had sex.

"Eric, fuck this pussy fuck it like you love it!"

I couldn't say too much with Brandon's dick in my mouth, but I made sure I didn't let that stop me from drilling Michelle into the mattress. I felt like I had my personal cheering section when Brandon started talking.

"Go ahead Eric. Fuck that fat pussy. It's good ain't it?"

Every so often Michelle would pull away from my dick,

turn around, and suck her wetness off of me. Whenever she did that it sent me over the edge. After a long while of me hitting Michelle doggy style, I was in the mood for something else. I lay on my back and flung my legs into the air. Brandon knew exactly what I wanted. He got between my legs and pushed his fat dick into my ass. Michelle walked over and sat on my face. She bounced up and down on my tongue as Brandon fucked my ass. My face was covered with Michelle's ass. I had to lift her up a few time 'cause I couldn't breathe. If I was going to die, I wanted it to be at that moment. In my mind I was already in heaven. Michelle got on her hands and knees and Brandon got behind her and slowly pushed his way into her ass. I was still under Michelle so I had the perfect view. I watched as her butt hole stretched to fit all of him in. His balls fell into my waiting mouth once he was all the way in her butt. I sucked his balls as he fucked her ass.

Michelle moaned louder than Brandon and I put together. The way our bodies intertwined was magical. I wiggled my way completely under Michelle to where we were face to face with Brandon still pounding her ass. I maneuvered my hard on until I felt the wet lips of her pussy suck me in. I could feel Brandon's dick going in and out of her as I pushed my way in. It felt like our dicks were rubbing together while they were inside of her. That alone was enough to get me off. I looked in the mirror on the wall of the room. I watched as Brandon and I both had our way with her. It was like watching a really good porn movie.

Michelle's large round breasts slapped up against my face as we both had our way. I sucked each of her erect nipples every time one swung near my mouth. I felt Brandon quicken his pace a little. I knew what was coming next. I can tell when he's ready to explode. His body tightens up and he starts stroking really fast.

"Which one of ya'll want the nut?" Brandon asked, as he pulled his dick out of Michelle and stroked it, waiting to see who was going to receive his cum. I damn near tossed Michelle on the floor getting my face right where it needed to be in order to catch all of his offering. Michelle pushed me out of the way so her breast could get splattered with his cream. In the end, my face and her tits were covered with Brandon's warm cum. I licked Michelle's face to make sure I got all of it in my mouth. I stroked my dick with excitement, as I tasted his salty cum.

Finally, it was my turn. I didn't even ask the question of who wanted it. I aimed my erect dick right at Brandon. He opened his mouth and waited on me to start shooting. My body tensed up as I shot a stream of sticky cum right over his mouth and onto his face. Stream after stream of cum flew from my body as I stroked myself frantically. I fell onto the bed as Michelle fell on top of me. Brandon stood over both of us laughing.

"What's so funny?" I asked as I looked up at him

"I just never thought I would have the opportunity to do both of you."

Michelle spoke up. "I hope ya'll don't think we're done. Shit, I'm just getting warmed up."

Brandon and I looked at each other and snickered as Michelle wiggled her ass in the air, hoping that one of us would jump on.

Strangely, I didn't feel guilty for sleeping with Brandon. I knew that Tracy was in a bad situation and I'm at home having sex with her man and her roommate. Most people would say that's kind of low, but I call it taking advantage of an opportunity.

We all lay in a sticky heap without saying a word at first. Then, of course, Michelle broke the ice. "Well, hell naw, I don't feel bad about fucking you Brandon."

We all looked at one another, and she continued. "I was gonna get mine. Since she's locked up for killing Professor Caldwell, it don't make sense to me to let her man's good dick get dusty."

Brandon spoke up. "Well, I don't think she did it. She's not that type of person."

"You didn't think she was the type to cheat on you either but she did that huh!" Michelle was beside herself. I guess Brandon sticking up for Tracy was more than she could handle. She continued. "I got tapes of her fucking him in the front room! I hope the cops come back around here I'm gonna give them the tapes and sing like a fucking bird!"

I didn't know what to say I had no idea that Tracy was still sleeping with Caldwell. I looked at Brandon and he didn't look upset at all by Michelle's comments. Then it hit me. "You knew she was still sleeping with him Brandon?"

He gave me a cold stare and started speaking. "Yeah I knew

about it. Your girl Michelle here confirmed it the last time I was here. I know she still has a thing for him. That's why she moved here to get to be with him while I was still in Miami. When I first came here with her I thought everything was cool but when Michelle told me everything that was going on I knew that she really didn't love me. I tried to tell her that Byron wasn't shit, but she wouldn't listen. She never knew I fucked him before she did. If anything, she stole him from me. I'm glad his ass is dead. That muthafucka was about to mess up all my plans."

I sat up. "What plans?"

Just then another voice spoke. "Yeah, Brandon, tell me your plans!"

All of us turned around to see Tracy standing at the bedroom door with fire in her eyes.

"What the fuck is going on Brandon! Why are the three of you naked and what's this plan, Brandon!"

I think we all were shocked. I guess with Michelle running her mouth, we didn't hear Tracy come through the door. Michelle reached for the comforter to drape over her half naked body.

Tracy snatched the comforter away from Michelle. "Stay naked you fat bitch. Don't try to cover up now. Half the campus has seen your ass anyway."

I thought Michelle was going to snap, but she sat there and didn't open her mouth. I had never seen Tracy this mad before. I sat on the edge of the bed, scared to move. All three of us sat quiet as church mice.

Tracy looked at me. "And I thought you were my friend you fuckin' fag! I thought I could talk to you. I thought I could tell you anything." Then a strange look ran across her face. "Now I get it!" She stared me right in the eyes. "B is for Brandon, ain't it?"

I just dropped my head because I knew she had me.

"All this time you've been fucking my man. Eric, I knew fat ass over there was capable of some low shit, but I never thought you were that kind of person."

I wanted to say something, anything, but I couldn't bring myself to speak. For the first time during all of this, I feel guilty. I dropped my head in shame.

"Don't drop your fuckin' head!"

"Tracy I'm sorry. I'm so sorry"

"What the hell are you sorry for? I know you're sorry that your stankin' ass got caught. Were you sorry when you were sucking my man's dick? Were you sorry when ya'll were fucking. When did you actually feel sorry, Eric?"

Michelle finally managed to collect a bunch of nerves together and try to leave the room. Tracy grabbed her by the hair. "Get your fat ass back in here. Don't try to leave now!" Tracy flung Michelle on the bed. I thought I was going to see Michelle get the beat down she deserved. "You don't know how bad I want to fuck you up right now. I swear I'm mad enough to kill you right now."

Michelle took this opportunity to really piss Tracy off. "What! You gonna kill me like you killed Byron?"

CHAPTER 18

Tracy

The room went silent. I just stood there and looked at Michelle I thought, there is no way that bitch just said that to me. Before I could even think about it, I jumped on Michelle's chest and was hitting her as hard as I could in the face. I repeatedly slammed my fist into her head. She tried to push me off of her but I was latched on like a pit bull. I tried to scratch the skin off her fat face. "Say something else bitch! Say something else," I screamed, as I continued to pound my fist into Michelle's face and the side of her head.

After what seemed like hours I felt Eric grab me from behind. I thought he was holding me so Michelle can get up and kick my ass. Michelle, struggling to get up from the mattress finally got to her feet and started towards me. I kicked my legs to try and keep her away from me, since I couldn't break the hold Eric had on me. As Michelle tried to time my kicks as to when she was gonna try and get close enough to hit me I saw Brandon come up behind her grab her around her arms.

"You betta be glad your man's holding me, bitch!" Michelle said, as Brandon turned her away from me.

"Fuck you, fat slut!" I tried my best to break away from Eric. I wanted to finish kicking her ass. I had waited on this day for a long time. I think we both knew it was gonna come down to this, but I had no idea her sleeping with my man would be the breaking point. Eric walked me out of the room, still holding me. We went into the front room and he tossed me on the sofa like a rag doll. As soon as I hit the sofa I jumped right up and stood right in Eric's face. "I thought you were my friend! I thought you and I could talk about anything!" I don't know if I was mad at the fact that Eric was sleeping with my man, or if I was mad that Eric genuinely hurt me. I stared him directly in his eyes. He lowered his head and started to cry. "What the hell are you crying for?" I asked, as he sat on the sofa and put his head in his hands. "You crying and I'm the one that just walked in on my man getting fucked by another man!"

Eric looked up at me with tears running down his face. For a second I felt bad for him. I don't know why, but I did. I should have jumped on him like I did Michelle but mamma ain't raise no fool. He might be gay, but he's still a man, and most men hit hard.

"Tracy I'm sorry. I can't begin to tell you how sorry I am. It was just a lust thing for me."

I walked over to Eric and stood over him I reached out my hand to rub the back of his head when anger ran through me again. My outreached loving hand turned into a hard slap across the back of his head.

"Do you think I'm stupid!"

Eric grabbed his head and looked at me with disbelief in his eyes.

"You were walking around here calling him B for a while! You knew what you were doing! You knew this would hurt me, but did you care, no! All you could think about was getting your little nasty dick in my man! So save that, I'm so sorry, shit!"

Still holding the back of his head Eric finally said a few words to me. "Tracy, you're right. I fucked up. I knew what I was doing the entire time, and again, I'm sorry. But you mean to tell me that you had no idea that your man might be gay or bi, whatever he want to call it?"

I thought about that question for a while then answered, "Hell no! Do you think I would have stayed with him if I knew he liked men?"

"Well, he might be trying to get you back for sleeping with Byron."

Right then anger shot from my feet to my head. I walked over to Eric and slapped him right across the face. Eric jumped up and I closed my eyes and braced myself for a punch but it never happened. I opened my eyes and Eric was still standing there with his head turned in the direction of the slap. I took a few steps backwards with my eyes fixed on Eric. He just stood there like a statue. He didn't move and he didn't speak a word. I figured this would be a good time for me to go kick Brandon's ass a little.

I walked back into Eric's bedroom where Michelle and Brandon were. As I stood to the door, I saw Brandon consoling Michelle. All I could see was her still swollen face, lying on my man's shoulder.

"Damn bitch, you still at it huh? You are just determined to get with my man!"

She looked up, and saw me coming right at her. She tried to hurry to her feet but I guess her weight shifted and she fell back as she tried to stand. By the time she hit the ground, I was standing over her, kicking her in the side and anyplace else my foot could find. This was gonna be an ass whippin' she was gonna remember for a long time. Eric heard her screaming and ran in the room. Brandon had walked to the other side of the room and watched as I kicked the hell out of her. Eric ran in and pushed me on the bed and helped Michelle up and walked her out of the room.

"I'ma whip your ass bitch! You wait, I got something for ya!" Michelle screamed as Eric pulled her out the room. She kicked and yelled all the way into the front room. All I could hear was her constant yelling about how she had something for me and how I was gonna get mine.

I turned my attention to Brandon. The love of my life. The man I wanted to marry. The man that my family loves so much. The man that I've been with since forever. He was standing on the other side of the bed from me, looking like a lost child. I wanted to cry, but anger kept that from happening. "What the hell are you thinking Brandon!" He just stood there with the dumbest damn look on his face. I could tell his mind was working overtime to come up with a good lie to tell me.

"See, what had happened was that..." From the first six words of that sentence, I knew bullshit was following.

"Just stop right there. Let me save you from telling a damn lie!" His mouth closed, as he knew I was on to him. He walked around the room, looking for his clothes. Like everything was all-good. My emotions got the best of me when he acted as if everything was fine.

"What the fuck's your problem Brandon? We were supposed to get married. We were supposed to be in love. How could you do this to me? And what hurt most of all is that you did this with my roommates!"

He kept picking up his clothes never once acknowledging me. At that point I lost all control.

"Brandon, talk to me damn it! I just caught you fucking another man and you're not going to say anything about it!"

Brandon swung around with a hate filled look on his face. "You caused this Tracy! Remember when you cheated on me back in Miami. How the fuck do you think I felt. He was my teacher, Tracy. He was my mentor. I looked up to him and you knew that, but that didn't stop you from sleeping with him did it!"

I was stunned. He turned it back on me. I was speechless. Then it hit me. The conversation Michelle and I had in the car that day when she asked me if I thought Brandon had really forgiven me for cheating on him. I though, that dirty bitch knew all along what was going on and didn't tell me. She played me the entire time.

"Yeah Tracy, it don't feel so good to be cheated on, does it! Then to make matters worse you came up here and cheated with him again. You left the state to come up here and cheat, this time without me finding out about it. You got the nerve to stand here and judge me! You running around calling people sluts, but look at you! Look at yourself for a second!"

Normally, if Brandon and I got into it, he knew just what to say to break me down. I am a ball of jell-o when it comes to him. I knew I had to stand strong, if not, the situation would only get worse for me.

"Yeah I cheated on you, but at least I cheated with the opposite sex. Tell me something, when did you become a fag?" I balled up my fist because I just knew he was going to come at me for that comment. His eyes tightened. His fist clenched but he didn't make a move towards me. I don't know what made me start going off, but I could not control myself. "That's why I cheated on you in the first place. I needed a real man. A man that could make me feels good. Not a man that wanted me to fuck him up his ass. Hell, all you had to do was ask me, I would have got a strap on and tore your ass up if that's what you wanted."

At this point, all I wanted to do was hurt him. I wanted him to feel the pain that I was feeling at that moment. I said things I knew weren't true, but I wanted to hurt his feelings, his manhood, anything I could.

"You know what Tracy, I would expect you to say something like that, I really would."

"Why is that?"

"Because if you'll kill a man, there is no depth to which you won't sink."

My eyes widened and filled with water. Tears started rolling down my face, but not because I was hurt by his words, but because of anger. I felt my hands start to tremble. I wanted to grab his throat and squeeze till my fingers crushed his esophagus.

"You dirty muthafucka," I said, in a cold, low tone. "You know damn well I could never kill anybody. But I am mad enough right now to damn sure try to kill you."

A nasty smile made its way across his face. He chuckled a little

"What the fuck is so funny!" I yelled, irately.

He walked over to me and whispered, "I know you didn't kill him. But all the fingers are pointed at you huh?"

A sick feeling came over me. I was confused and couldn't speak.

"Let me break it down for you." He sat on the edge of the bed and began his story. "I killed Byron."

My mouth fell open. There was no way under the sun I was in love with a person that could do such a thing.

He continued. "Michelle told me that the two of you were still getting together. I wanted you all to myself. Obviously you felt differently than I did. So, Michelle told me where his class was and what kind of car he drove and I waited on him to show up for work.

"When he pulled into the parking lot, I quickly pulled up

next to him. The funny part was he was actually happy to see me. It was like old times again. As he got out his car, I walked over to him and threw one arm over his shoulder to hug him and I shoved a knife into his stomach. I placed my hand over his mouth and shoved him back into the car. I began to stab him repeatedly in the chest. I don't know how many times I stabbed him, but when I was finished there was blood everywhere.

"To my surprise, not a single soul was in the parking lot at that time. I guess that was a sign that it was his time to go. 'Cause you know in movies and books it's always somebody that just happened to see you right before you're done and walking away."

I was dumbfounded. I didn't know what to say. I didn't know what to do. All I could do was sit there and stare at him. "I killed him for us."

"For us? What the hell are you talking about?"

"I took him out of our lives forever. It can be just you and me now baby."

"Hell no it can't! You killed somebody. You took a life. Somebody's son is no longer here because of you, and you think that I'm silly enough to want you after all of that? Ride or die chick, my ass. I ain't one of them."

He looked at me with a very disturbing look. I knew nothing good was about to come out of his mouth. "Fine then. I guess your ass will fry for his murder. Don't forget, you're still the primary suspect. And when I tell them how you killed him because he was about to tell your boyfriend that ya'll were sleeping together, and when Michelle shows them the tape she has of ya'll fuckin' in the front room a few days ago, oh, I'll say it's an open and shut case. But it doesn't have to end like this for us. Marry me and I'll make it all go away."

I almost passed out. "What did you just say? Marry you?"

"Yes."

"Hell no!"

"Have it your way, dumb ass!" Brandon turned to walk out of the room. He stopped at the door and looked at me. "Oh yeah, before I forget, I'll make sure the murder weapon is found somewhere in this house after the police come and take your ass to jail."

CHAPTER 19

Michelle

"That bitch don't know who she's fuckin' with." I couldn't help but walk around screaming at the top of my lungs. Not only did she attack me but she scratched up my face. Eric and I walked into my room so I could put on some clothes. I sat on the edge of my bed and decided it was time to put Miss Thing away for a while. I reached for the phone. Eric stopped me before I could pick it up.

"Who are you about to call?"

"The police!" I tried to reach for the phone again but he stopped me again.

"Why are you gonna get them involved?"

"That ho just attacked me. Look at my face. I have swelling and scratches everywhere, and you don't think I should press charges?"

"You were fucking her man! She was supposed to kick your ass!"

"Well, I was the only one that got attacked. If I remember it correctly, there was three naked people in that bed not just one!" With that, I pushed Eric's hand off the phone and started dialing the number.

He looked at me like he wanted to knock the phone out of my hand. I'm sure he actually thought about doing it for a second, but his good judgment got to him.

The 911 operator picked up the line. "911, is this an emergency?"

"Yes, I was just attacked by my roommate." I tried to sound if I was distraught and crying. My voice trembled as I spoke.

"Police are on the way, is your roommate still there?"

"Yes, she's in the next room. Please tell them to hurry. I don't know if she's coming back in my room. Please hurry up!"

Now getting dressed, Eric stood in my doorway and watched my Oscar Award winning performance. I was so good, I even had a few tears drop from my eyes to fool myself. I put my hand over the phone so the 911 operator couldn't hear what I was telling Eric. That bitch got this coming to her ass. I told her a long time ago I'll fuck her up if she ever crossed me.

A few minuets later, we heard a knock at the door. I started talking to the operator again. "I think the police are here now," I said, voice still shaking.

"Okay. If you need any further assistance, call me back."

"Thank you so much. You've been a great help."

I hung up the phone and walked to the door. I looked out the peephole, and sure enough, two police officers were standing there.

Eric, walking next to me, asked, "You can't be serious about this?"

"Shit, 'bout to get a whole lot worse for old girl in a second." When I opened the door the two cops immediately saw the scratches and the bruises on my face.

"Are you all right Miss?" One of the officers asked, while the other one walked into the house to look around.

I had gone back into character for the police. The voice was trembling again. The tears were flowing it was beautiful. "No officer, I'm not okay. My roommate just jumped on me. She hit me from behind and got on top of me, pinned my arms under my body, and proceeded to punch and scratch me in the face."

"Is this gentleman your roommate?"

He looked at Eric and placed his hands on his handcuffs.

"Yes sir, he is my roommate, but not the one that jumped on me. She's in the other room."

The other police officer walked to Tracy's room and knocked on the door.

"Police, is anybody in there?"

I heard the door open.

"Please step into the front room," the officer ordered.

Brandon and Tracy both walked into the front room where Eric and I were already sitting on the sofa. I made a few more tears roll down my face for the added effect it would have on the police. As if the mere sight of her made me break down with fear.

One officer took me in the kitchen while the other stepped outside with Tracy.

The officer I was with was so sweet and caring. He was professional. I felt like he had my safety as his main concern. "So tell me what happened," he asked me as I sat to the kitchen table.

I broke down again to make sure he knew I was hurting. Taking short quick breaths and with tears flowing, I said, "I'm so scared right now. I don't know if I did the right thing by calling you."

"Why are you scared?"

"Because I know she's going to come after me again."

"Why did she come after you the first time?"

"Because I found out that she killed Byron Caldwell."

"That's the guy that was murdered this morning isn't it?"

"Yes." I knew I had the officer right where I wanted him. With these bruises on my face and a still-hot murder case, I knew almost anything I said would be enough for them to put her away.

"Are you telling me that your roommate murdered Mr. Caldwell?"

"That's exactly what I'm telling you. She killed him because he was going to tell her family that they were sleeping together. He was so happy to have her; he wanted the world to know."

The officer was almost giddy. He knew he had a murder case in which he could say he solved. His eyes were bright, and all of a sudden he was Mr. Professional. All that caring stuff went right out the window.

"Did she confess this to you?"

"Yes she did. I found a tape of her and Byron making love right here in the front room. I didn't know she was behind me while I was watching it. She became irate with me. I was trying to find a blank tape to record my favorite soap opera on. She asked me why I was watching her have sex, and I told her it was a mistake. She began cursing me out about it. I thought we were just gonna get into a verbal altercation about it. I said a few words, I think something along the lines of, I know Byron's happy he don't have to put up with your silly ass anymore. I turned to walk away and that's when she hit me in the head. I fell to the ground and she turned me over, pinned my arms under me, and started hitting me in the face."

The officer looked like he was ready to burst at the seems, waiting on me to get to the confession part.

"I'm sorry you had to go through that, but did she confess to the murder?"

"Yes. When she was on top of me she said I should kill your ass the same way I killed Byron."

"Did anyone else hear her say this to you?"

I looked up and behind the officer was Brandon walking up. He was nodding his head in a yes motion.

"Yes sir, her boyfriend heard her say it."

"Her boyfriend? Is he still here?"

"Yes, he's right over there."

I pointed to Brandon who was standing in the entranceway to the kitchen.

"Are you the boyfriend?"

"Yes sir."

"Tell me what happened."

Brandon looked at me and started telling his version "Well, when I walked in, Tracy was already on top of Michelle. At first I kinda just stood and watched. You know, being a guy, you always want to see two women fight just in case a titty pops out or something."

The officer and I both smirked a little and let Brandon get back to telling his story. "I saw Tracy starting to really inflict some punishment to Michelle's face, so I decided to put an end to the fight. I reached down to grab Tracy when I heard her say. I should kill you like I killed Byron.

I guess that was all the officer needed to hear. About the time we were wrapping up in the kitchen Tracy and the other officer were walking back in the house. We all stood on separate sides of the front room while the two officers talked to one another. I was standing next to Brandon and, Tracy and Eric were standing together.

Tracy looked over at me "Damn, I hate you," she said.

The officers turned around and looked her right in the eyes and walked over to her. "Please turn around and put your hands on your head."

Tracy's mouth fell open. I looked at Eric and his was wide open as well. The officer repeated himself. This time Tracy did as she was told.

As he pulled his handcuffs from his belt, he told Tracy the charges against her. "You are under arrest for Aggravated Battery and for the murder of Byron Caldwell."

Tracy spun around with one arm in the handcuffs "I didn't murder anybody! What the fuck are you talking about?"

The officer tried to turn her back around so he could get the other cuff on her. Tracy tried to pull away as she pleaded her case. "This is bullshit. I didn't kill anybody. Brandon killed Byron!"

We all stood and watched as the police had to throw Tracy on the ground to get the other cuff on her. When they got the other cuff on, they read Tracy her rights as they walked her out the house. On the way out the door she constantly repeated herself "I didn't kill anybody, Brandon did it."

We all stood to the front door and watched as the police put Tracy in the police car and drive away. Eric turned to Brandon and I. "What did ya'll tell the police!"

"I told them the truth Eric," I said, as I went into the kitchen to get some ice for my swollen jaw.

Eric walked over to Brandon "You have to help her. Do you really believe that she killed Byron?"

Brandon dropped his head. "I don't know what to believe."

Eric paced around the house like a caged animal. After a while, watching him got on my nerves. "Eric what is your problem. Why are you walking around the house all upset when you were the one fucking her man first? Now you're all upset 'cause she's gone. What's the deal with you?"

Eric stopped and walked over to me. "Listen, I know I am just as wrong as anybody else for what I did, but she is up on murder charges. This is bigger than, why are you fucking my man, type shit. That girl could lose her life behind this."

"Then that's, that girl business. She should have thought of that before she did what she did."

Eric's face was filled with disgust. He went in his room and changed his clothes. When he came out, he put something on the entertainment center in the front room and walked out the house without saying a word to anybody.

Brandon and I sat on the sofa. I still had the ice on my jaw. He looked at me and burst into laughter.

"What's funny?" I asked.

"All she had to do was marry me, and this would have all been over. But she's the stupid type that doesn't know a good deal when they hear it."

"What do you mean?"

"Well, to be honest with you. I killed Byron."

I sat there in disbelief. When I told the police Tracy had killed him, I just wanted to make her life a little more difficult. I had no idea what really went on. I never left from the last time I was up here. I killed him to get him out the way of me getting a hold of Tracy's family's money. When I asked her to marry me and she said no, there was no longer a need for me to try to win her over. So, I figured if she could turn me down, I'll just pin the murder on her."

I didn't know what to say or do. For the first time, I was actually scared of Brandon. He looked at me with a huge smile on his face. "I guess now, it can be just you and I together forever." He grabbed my hand and led me to Tracy's bedroom. I was wearing a pair of shorts and a t-shirt and he had on just a pair of basketball shorts. He laid me on the bed and pulled off my shorts. I was finally going to get the man I wanted, but it just felt different. I felt like I didn't know this person. He rubbed my vagina with his fingers and I didn't get wet at all. Normally, I would have soaked the sheets with the first touch, but I was so scared, I couldn't get into it.

He stood in front of me and asked me to give him head. I opened my mouth and he almost choked me the way he shoved his dick in. My mind was racing one hundred miles a minute. I didn't want to be here at this moment. I wanted to be anywhere else but here right now with him. I didn't want to piss him off and have him try to kill me so I tried to calm down as much as possible. I tried to block everything out of my mind and just do it like I used to when I was to pay off my mothers' debts.

He pulled his dick out of my mouth and turned me around to enter me doggy style. I lay limp across the bed and let him have his way. I actually cried a little, I was so scared. Every now and then I would moan and "aaahh" a little to let him know he was hitting my spot. I had never wanted a man to be done so fast. He pulled my hair and I thought I was done for. I just knew the next thing I would feel would be a knife across my throat. But he was just trying to get himself off.

After a few minutes, he finally came. I was so happy that he was done. I stood up and went into the bathroom to clean up. I locked the door behind me. I stood in the mirror and hated the person that was looking back at me. I had told a bold face lie to the police that may have ended the life of an innocent person. I had no idea what Brandon had really done. But one thing was weighing heavy on my mind. I opened the bathroom door to ask Brandon a question. "Brandon, were you at the mall earlier?"

"Yeah, why?"

"No reason. I was there and thought I saw somebody that looked just like you."

CHAPTER 20

Eric

Right about now, I feel horrible. I was caught in bed with my friends' man and now she's up on murder charges. I don't know how to help her or where to begin if I wanted to help her. I could call her family and let them know what's going on. But that will only get them in a panic. I know my girl is innocent, but I have no way of proving it right now. All I can do now is hope that somebody said something in the front room that I can use to get my girl out of jail. As I drove around trying to figure out a way to clear Tracy's name, my cell phone rang.

"Hello?"

"Eric this is Michelle," she said in a whisper.

"What's wrong? Why are you whispering?"

"Brandon is in the shower right now. He killed Byron."

I almost ran off the road. I pulled over on the side of the street and put the car in park. "What did you just say?"

"It was Brandon that killed Byron. He admitted it to me a few minutes ago."

"Are you sure that's what he said?"

"Damn man, yes, that's what he said."

"I'm on my way home right now. Just chill till I get there."

I hung up the phone, made a u-turn in the middle of the street, and raced back home. I had to have run about ten red lights, but I could not leave another friend at home with Brandon, for him to do whatever to her. I didn't know what I was going to do when I got to the house. All I knew is, that I didn't want her alone with him.

My heart raced as I turned on our street. I didn't know

what I was going to see when I opened the front door. My keys hit the lock and I heard a little movement. I swung open the door and Brandon was on the sofa and Michelle was sitting across from him in the recliner. I walked over to the entertainment center and tossed my car keys on top and grabbed what I had put up there earlier. I turned to Brandon. "Can we talk in my room?"

"Sure."

He got up and followed me in the bedroom. He grabbed me around my waist as the door closed behind him. He pressed his growing manhood into my jean-covered butt.

"Before you get yourself all worked up Mr. Man. Tell me again what you told the police about Tracy."

He kissed me on my neck and rubbed my stomach. "Come on, tell me boo. Do you really think Tracy had anything to do with Byron's death?"

"To be honest, no. But your girl Michelle did tell me that she had a lot to do with it."

I turned and looked at him, eye to eye. "What did she have to do with it?"

"Everything, she helped Tracy do it."

I was thrown for a loop. I didn't expect him to say that. I know Michelle has her ways, but I didn't think she was a murderer. Somebody was lying. Michelle said Brandon did it, and Brandon said Michelle did it. To be honest, neither can be trusted. Brandon continued. "You know what else she told me," he said, as he unbuttoned my shirt and rubbed my chest.

"What?"

"She said the knife she stabbed him with is under her bed. In a plastic bag."

I pulled away from Brandon. And just stared at him for a second.

"Are you sure that's what she said to you?"

"Yes baby, why would I lie to you?"

As soon as he said that I started thinking that Michelle was the one telling the truth. One thing I know is that when a person says why would I lie or, trust me, right then, you know some funny stuff is going on.

I walked away from Brandon and went to the bedroom door.

"Where are you going? I thought we were gonna get something going here?"

I turned and looked at him. "Naw, I want to go talk to Michelle about this situation."

"Are you crazy. All she's gonna do is deny it and blame it on somebody else."

"So what do you think we should do?" I really wanted to know what was on his mind.

"I think we should call the police, get them over here, show them where the murder weapon is, and get her locked up too."

I had no idea Brandon was this kind of person. It's hard to believe that I gave myself to him, wanted to be with him, hurt a friend for him. But then something hit me.

"You really don't seem too upset that Tracy is locked up."

"Well, I'm kinda hurt that she moved all the way up here and moved Caldwell up here with her. She was still sleeping with him. That hurt."

I do see his point. I've also seen how Michelle and Tracy started getting along right before all this went down.

"Eric, we need to call the police and have them come get Michelle. She helped Tracy kill Byron. We both know that. The murder weapon is in her room. We need to get them over here before she moves the knife."

I didn't want to believe him but he was making good sense to me. I walked to the other side of the room where the phone was. I stared at it for a second them reached for it. As soon as my hand touched the phone it rang.

"Hello?"

"You have a collect call from the Pitt County Jail," an automated voice said.

Then I heard a very sad and scared voice say, "Tracy."

My hands started to shake. I didn't want to let on that Tracy was on the phone to Brandon, so I calmed myself down and tried to talk normal.

"Will you accept the charges?"

Calmly, I answered, "Yes."

I felt Brandon pulling at my shirtsleeve "Who is that?"

"A friend! Damn, chill out."

I focused back on the phone call, "Hey wuz up man?"

"Eric, I know I said some hateful stuff to you today, but you know I didn't kill anybody." Tracy's voice sounded like a beaten woman. Her voice was tired and lazy.

"So what you need me to do playa?"

"Brandon must be in the room with you huh?"

"Yeah, so what else you need?" I looked back at Brandon and he seemed to be okay, thinking that I was on the phone with a friend.

"Brandon killed Byron. I know that may be hard to believe, but he did. I need you to believe me."

"I do. You're not the first person to say that."

"He must have told you or Michelle too, then. He's a big mouth. He likes to brag about anything he does."

"I feel you."

"I told the police he did it, so they might be around there to question ya'll."

In the background, I heard someone yell, "Time!"

"Eric, I gotta go, but get him to confess!"

After that the phone went dead, I hung up and went and sat next to Brandon on the bed. I wrapped my arm around him and asked, "Have you ever done something and just had to tell somebody."

He looked at me with a confused squint on his face.

"What the hell are you talking about?"

"I just want you to know that you can tell me anything. I love you and I want to be with you."

"That's good to know."

I had to say something to get him to confess. "Feel free to tell me anything your heart desires," I said, as I rubbed his back, running my finger up and down his spine.

"Well, there is something."

I sat up straight. He had my full attention

"I slept with Byron a few weeks before he and Tracy met."

I just sat there looking dumb. I didn't know what to say. That was the last thing I thought I'd hear him say.

"You slept with Byron?"

"Yes. He was my teacher back home. He tutored me after class. Eventually, one thing led to another, and before you know it, we were at his house in bed."

I couldn't close my mouth. I was floored by what I was hearing. This entire situation got stranger and stranger by the second. "So you think Tracy and Michelle killed him because…?" I asked, hoping to pull more information out of him.

"Because, neither of them could have him. He was mine. He was only sleeping with Tracy to get at me for breaking it off with him. We all know Michelle is a slut. Look what she did with us. She even told me that she had a thing for Byron last time I was here."

I stood up and walked to the door.

"Then we need to go to the police station, tell them what we know, and get both of them locked up for a very long time."

Brandon stood up and hugged me. He pressed against my pocket and we heard a loud click noise. Brandon stood back from me. "What was that?"

"I don't know. Sounds like my leg popped," I said, shaking my leg like it had slipped out of place. I had completely forgotten I had a mini voice recorder in my pocket that I had put on the entertainment center before I left, just to see if somebody would say anything that might clear Tracy.

Brandon and I walked to the front door. Michelle looked at us and asked, "Where are ya'll going?"

"We'll be right back," I said as I opened the door. Brandon went out the door in front of me. I looked back at Michelle and winked at her. She just dropped her head.

On the way over to the police station, Brandon told me all about his encounters with Byron. I was sure he had killed Byron at this point. He thought I was buying into all his bullshit he was tossing around. The only thing he said I believed was that he slept with Byron.

Once at the station, we walked in and saw several people

that looked like they needed a bath desperately. The smell in the station was an old shoe type smell. I tried to breathe as little as possible, hoping not to poison my insides with the smell. We walked up to the front desk where a heavy set lady that looked like a man with a beard raised her head from the newspaper and asked us what we were there for.

"We're here because we have information about the Byron Caldwell murder," I said.

In a very deep husky voice she said, "Ya'll sit right there. I'll get the detective to see you in a minute."

The bearded lady picked up the phone and Brandon leaned over to me. "Look, we have to be on the same page. Just tell them that the murder weapon is in the house and that Tracy and Michelle killed Byron. Tell them that Michelle confessed to us while they took Tracy and put her in the police car. Tell them that all the crying that Michelle was doing at the house was all phony. She helped kill Professor Caldwell."

I wanted to jump up and knock his head off. This bastard was trying to get me to go along with turning in two innocent people for something he did. But in front of him, I played along.

"You know Eric, when we walk out of here, it will just be you and I together forever. I love you."

It took everything in me not to throw up. I looked him square in the eyes. "I love you too baby."

Two gentlemen in nice black suits walked over and introduced themselves as the detectives on the case. One asked me to go with him and the other asked Brandon to follow him. I walked into this small room and sat to a table. The detective walked in. "Would you like something to drink sir?"

"No, I'm fine."

"So I hear you have some information about a murder that I'm investigating?"

"Yes I do."

"Tell me what you know."

I took a deep breath and began telling everything I knew about the case.

"Well I have been told three different stories. I was told

that Tracy killed Byron. Then I was told Michelle killed Byron."

"Who told you Michelle killed him?"

"Brandon, the guy I walked in here with."

"How does he know?"

"He said Michelle told him."

"Have you talked to Michelle?"

"Yes, and she told me Brandon killed Byron."

The detective seemed like he was more confused listening to me, than I was telling it to him.

"Well son, let me tell you. We went over to Mr. Caldwell's house and did a little digging over there and it seems like your friend Tracy was over there the night before he was murdered. We also talked to an eye witness that said they saw Tracy running from his house, jumping in her car, and speeding off down the street."

I didn't know all of this had happened. Maybe Tracy really did have something to do with his murder. "Sir, I don't know anything about all that. But, what I do know is that the murder weapon is said to be in our house."

"Really, where?"

"In Michelle's room. I don't know who killed Mr. Caldwell, but I don't think it was Tracy."

"So you think it was Michelle then?"

"No, I didn't say that."

The detective got really upset and started yelling at me. "You said the murder weapon is in Michelle's room. You also said that Brandon told you that Michelle confessed to the killing. These are your words, correct?"

"Yes but…"

"So you are saying that Michelle is the murderer!"

"No!" I jumped up out of my seat, and my pocket with the recorder in it hit the table.

Then it dawned on me that I had something recorded. I didn't know what it was, but we were going to listen to it right now. Either this tape is gonna prove that Tracy really did it or somebody else is going down for the murder.

"Can I reach in my pocket sir?"

"For what?"

"I forgot I have a recorder that I set up in the house earlier today to record if someone confessed."

"Give it to me." The detective's eyes widened and a smile shot across his face for a split second. He rewound the tape and pressed play. The detective and I both sat still as we listened to Brandon confess to Michelle that he was the one that killed Byron. I'm not sure if I was surprised or not because Brandon had already showed me the kind of person he really was. We also heard the conversation that Brandon and I had where he was telling me about how he and Byron were ex-lovers.

"That little shit," the detective said as he swung open the door to the room we were in. I heard him yelling down the hall. "Where is Brandon!"

I heard another voice. "He left about five minuets ago sir." The detective came back to where I was.

"Where would he be going?"

"I don't know. Maybe back to Miami."

The detective left the room in a hurry. A few seconds later another officer walked in the room where I was and asked me to follow him. We walked back to the front of the station. The officer turned to me "Sit down and wait here."

I sat there in that one spot for what seemed like an hour. Finally, I heard a female scream.

"Eric!"

I jumped and turned to see Tracy running towards me. I hugged her tight. We both started to cry as we held one another.

"They let you out?"

"Yeah, they said they had a confession on tape and that they were going to arrest the real killer."

We held hands as we walked out of the station. I hadn't told Tracy everything that Brandon told me. I wanted to wait till we got home and she got herself together. As we pulled up to our house cops were everywhere. All I could think is that Brandon had gotten to Michelle before anybody could get to him.

CHAPTER 21

Michelle

If I had known the kind of person Brandon is I would never have gotten involved with him. I walked around the front room of the house, trying to figure out my next move. I'm not resting easy with the idea that Brandon and Eric left here together. Something tells me I'm gonna come up on the short end of whatever they're planning.

Suddenly, there was a frantic knocking at the door. I jumped up and ran to the window to see who it was. It was Brandon breathing heavy and looking around over both shoulders. I didn't want to answer the door but the way he was knocking on the door, it was either open it or he was going to break it down. I opened the door and without saying a word Brandon rushed past me.

"Brandon what's wrong?" I asked as he went into Eric's room and grabbed his things.

"Nothing!" He didn't say a word as he flung his bags into his car and backed out the driveway. It didn't take him two minutes to grab all his things and be gone. I stood to the door and watched as he spun his wheels and sped off down the street.

I didn't know what was going on. I sat in the front room and tried to calm my nerves by watching a little television, but soon that was disturbed by the sound of screeching tires in the front of the house. Again I jumped up and ran to the window. My eyes almost fell from my face when I looked out and saw four police cars parked in the driveway, the yard, and on the street. It was police everywhere. I squatted down next to the front door. I didn't know if they were going to start shooting or what was going to happen. Then it dawned on me that Brandon and Eric must have gone to the police station and told them that I was the one that killed Byron. How could they do that to me! Well they have another thing coming if they think for a fucking second I'm going to go out like a sucka. My mama ain't raise no punk!"

I went into the kitchen to find anything sharp. "One of them come up in here, his ass getting cut!" I'm not gonna lie, I was scared as all outdoors. My heart was beating fast. My palms were wet. I felt like Malcolm X peeking through the blinds, protecting himself. Only difference is he had a rifle and I have a butcher knife. I saw a shadowed figure walk past the back glass door. I felt like I was in a movie. But just like in the movies, there's always a way out. Well, I obviously didn't get my script 'cause there is no way out that I can see. The two of them sold me out to the police. To protect Brandon, Eric turned on me.

I looked out the window again and saw half the neighborhood standing outside trying to figure out why all the police were at the house. I felt like I was surrounded. A few minutes later I noticed I hadn't locked the door from when Brandon left. I slowly walked over to the door as soon as my hand touched the knob the door pushed open. Without thinking I swung the knife I had in my hand. I cut an unsuspecting officer right across the chest. I stood there in shock as the officer stumbled back out the door. I looked up and saw several other officers rushing towards the door. I had not seen a single soul pull his gun out until I cut that cop.

"Get on the ground!" All the officers yelled at once. I panicked and threw the knife down and fell to my knees. A female officer grabbed me and pushed me face down on the carpet. The entire neighborhood was standing outside and saw the whole incident. They had me on the ground right in the front door. I heard someone say check the back room he might be in there.

"Who are ya'll looking for?" I asked, as they pulled me into a sitting position. The female officer got in my face and asked, "Where is Brandon?"

"What?" I don't know what I expected her to say to me, but that wasn't it.

"I said where is Brandon?"

"He left here a few minutes ago."

"Did he tell you where he was going?"

"No, he didn't say a word. He ran in and ran out."

Just then I saw Eric and Tracy walk into the house. They stood in the doorway, looking at me with disbelief. Eric spoke up first. "Please tell me you're not the reason that cop is being loaded into an ambulance?"

I just dropped my head, I was so scared. I got carried away. In my head the situation was a lot worse than it actually was. My imagination took over and made a movie scenario out of the situation.

I heard a voice behind me. "You have the right to remain silent. You have the right to an attorney. If you can not afford an attorney, one will be provided for you..."

I really stopped listening after that point. I felt numb. I really thought that at any moment I was going to wake up and this had all been a very bad dream.

"What am I being charged with officer? I asked as they marched me out the front door. I thought that the entire college was in my front yard. I looked around and saw several faces of people I knew, including Prentice. Now I hate that I treated him so bad. If we were still kicking it, I know he would come through for me, but now I don't know what I'm going to do.

"You're being charged with the attempted murder of a police officer."

I didn't look anybody in the face as the officer pressed my head down to make sure I was in the car. I closed my eyes as the police car slowly backed out the yard and went down the street.

* * *

A few months later I was in court. I looked around the courtroom and only saw two faces I knew: Eric and Tracy. I know that Tracy probably hates my guts, but she was there, and not as a person that came to gloat at my situation, but a person that came to make sure I was okay. They both smiled at me when I walked into the courtroom. For the first time in my life I felt like someone was there for me. I've never felt like that before. Anytime someone was around me they wanted something from me. Men always wanted to fuck me and women just wanted to get next to me to talk my business and hate on me.

I pleaded no contest to avoid any real time behind bars. I was sentenced to ten years in jail but I'll be up for parole in three. I really hate that a dick is the cause of all my problems. I never thought that a man would cause me to lose my damn mind like I did. I wanted to be with Brandon so bad, I betrayed a person that honestly never did a thing to me. I cut a police officer and ended up behind bars. A man is dead and I feel like I helped kill him. At night I try to blame Brandon for all my problems. I even blame my mom from time to time. If she had raised me better and not have me sucking dick and fucking all those guys I might have went another way. But I guess now is one of those times where you have to take responsibility for your own actions. I let myself get all caught up with a slimy ass nigga. He's running the street fucking up another woman's life and I'm sitting in here waiting to go to prison for a few years.

My stomach churned as the prison bus pulled up to the gate of the Nash Prison. All the inmates were out in the yard exercising and talking to one another. Within an hour I had been processed and was on my way to my cell. I sat on my bunk and tried to make myself as comfortable as possible. I looked up and there were four women inmates standing at the entrance to my cell.

"Wuz up?" I tried to sound all-hard but my heart was pounding. I had watched a lot of movies where they come in your cell and beat your ass for no apparent reason.

One of the women walked over to me. "Hey, you Michelle huh?"

"Yeah, why?" I know cutting an officer didn't get me the kind of reputation that had people wanting to hang out with me.

"You went to college in Greenville?"

"Yeah," I was starting to get a little scared. This woman knows who I am, but I have no clue who she is.

"You know a dude named Prentice?"

Now I'm really messed up. She knows me and Prentice. "Yeah I know him. We kicked it for a minute"

"You loved him?"

All off a sudden I felt a sharp pain in my stomach. I fell back on the bed. I clutched my stomach. Something was sticking out of it. I looked at my hands and they were covered with blood. I had been stabbed. I couldn't scream. I wanted to, but the sound would not come out. The woman that stabbed me stood over me and pulled the shank from my stomach and stabbed me again. I felt like I was falling asleep. The last thing I heard was, "That's my little brother bitch!"

CHAPTER 22

Eric

It's a shame what happened to my girl Michelle. She was a victim all her life and died that way as well. As Tracy and I stand here at her funeral, it just makes me think about all the good times we shared. The night at the club, the night we had at the party. I want to remember her as a good friend and a good person.

The relationship between Tracy and I has never been the same. We're cool, don't get me wrong, but the secrets we once shared are no more. We don't talk like we used to. I messed all of that up. I let sex come between a good friend and me. We try to stay out of each other's way when we're home at the same time. This year has been full of ups and downs. I tried to get all A's in my classes since my roommate died, but I found out that was only an urban legend.

The only person I actually talk to from time to time is Skye. She still wants to get in a serious relationship with me. I wouldn't mind being with her, except I don't trust myself anymore. I feel like I will only hurt her somewhere down the road. She needs a person that will cherish her the way she deserves. I'm not that person.

Christmas break is right around the corner and I have to go back home. My relationship with my family is as bad as ever. I really don't want to go, but I have nowhere else to hang out for a week and a half. I guess I have to go home and endure the comments my family is sure to make. I have to sit back and listen to my brothers call me a faggot and watch my father's look of disgust.

I don't think I'm going to move back into this house after the holiday break. I don't think I can live here, knowing that my life changed in this house. I have a memory that will haunt me forever because of my actions in this house.

If I've learned nothing else, I've learned that real friends are hard to find, but easy to lose. No matter how good the sex might be with someone, it's not worth loosing a good friend over. Living with the fact that I destroyed a life for it, is what kills me the most. It kinda reminds me of something my mother used to always say when we were growing up it's all fun and games till somebody gets hurt. I always thought she was talking about horse playing but I guess she was really talking about life. I played games and had a lot of fun, but in the end somebody got hurt.

CHAPTER 23

Tracy

I can't believe that my life has turned out this way. Eric and I barely speak to each other. He's cool and all, but he hurt me more than anything else. I really felt at ease with him. He destroyed all that for me by sleeping with Brandon.

Speaking of Brandon, my father sent me a copy of the Miami Herald today and on the front page was a picture of Brandon being led away in handcuffs. The story said that he was wanted for murder and he was found in his girlfriend's apartment. Evidently, he was running his mouth to somebody down there, telling them what went on up here and they went back and told the police. He's looking at forty-five years in prison.

I don't think he really knows what he did. He's the reason Michelle is dead. He's the reason that Eric and I don't really talk. He's the reason Byron is dead. He's the reason. He touched so many lives in a negative way. It's hard to believe I actually loved that fool. But hey, you know what they say, hindsight is 20/20.

I now see things in him that I should have seen a long time ago. His quick temper. I thought it meant that he didn't take any crap from anybody. That was a turn on for me. It felt good to run around and say that my man got a quick temper, trying to make other people fear him. How stupid was I. His cute quick temper turned into an awful murder.

I remembered several times when we would argue, he would grab my arms. He wouldn't hit me, but he would scare the hell out of me when he did it. I took that as a sign of I better not piss him off. Those again, made me feel like my man was a man. A real man takes control of his woman when she's flying off at the lip. Damn, just to think about it makes me embarrassed. I should have walked then, but I didn't. Something about him being mad and getting all crazy was a turn on for me. The sex was great when he was pissed off. But then again, I guess that's what got me in this mess in the first place. Sex.

In the end, everybody was having sex with my man but me. I had no idea that he was into men. That caught me totally off guard. Now I see what the old folks mean when they say you betta know who you layin' up with. I see now, I didn't know Brandon as well as I thought I did. Sure, I knew his favorite color, drink, car, and rap artist, but I really didn't know him. Well, I take that back. I knew him, but I closed my eyes to that side of him.

My father told me he would rent the entire house for me so I wouldn't have to have any roommates again. That's a good thing. The only thing is that I have someone moving in with me that my parents don't know about. He has been my rock throughout this entire ordeal. He has also been my lover for the past few weeks. He's the type of man that I'm really drawn to. A man that took care of my problem for me. A man that made it all go away when I needed it too.

As I sit in the front room of my house I see my mans' car pull up outside. I can't help but smile as he gets out of the car and he's wearing the Hilfiger button down and khakis I love so much. I guess everybody would freak out if they knew Prentice had Michelle killed in prison. The girl who killed her wasn't even his sister, just some crack fiend that was in jail and he gave her a few hundred dollars to take Michelle out. That showed me that he is a man of his word. He told Michelle she was going to get hers and I guess she did.

I told him how much Brandon had hurt and used me. So he had one of his friends that lives in Miami go to a bar that I knew Brandon hung out at and seduce him into running his damn mouth, which he did, and got his ass busted for it.

If you're wondering about Eric, he's next on the list. We haven't thought of a way to get his ass, but we will. And when we do, it's gonna be good as hell. But for right now, my punk ass man Prentice, as Michelle liked to call him, has a hard dick and it's my job to make it soft again. I love a clean-cut scandalous ass nigga.

The End

Featured Excerpt

From the Essence Best Seller

When it goes beyond curiosity...

Swingers

Torrian Ferguson

Chapter 1

Greg's Eyes

I really didn't know what to think when my wife, Rena, agreed to bringing a third party into our bedroom.

At first, when it was suggested to us, I wasn't quite fond of the idea, but about five minutes later, it started to click . . .if I had two women in my bed then I would have two pussies staring me in the face; one ready to be eaten and the other one ready, willing and able to be dived into. That's when I said, 'Gregory Robbins, *you gotta be the mother fuckin' man!*'

At that point I agreed to swing . But don't be mistaken, I'm all for bringing another woman into the bed I share with my wife, but the idea of another man laying next to me, stank ass and hairy balls, turned me off. Not to mention that I would probably lose it if he tried to hit my wife off. That was something I didn't want to think about let alone be apart of.

You must understand that I'm a man, a heterosexual man; who for most of my adult life, has had the good fortune of having any woman that I've wanted, which I guess caused a lot of insecurities and problems for my wife. Seeing that I didn't want her to suffer any more (and me being the good husband that I am) I decided to give her exactly what the doctor ordered, with just one catch . . .we could only get our freak on with bisexual *women.*

Rena, being the loving wife that she is, was simply too happy to agree. Besides, she probably figured that if I slept with other women in front of her, she wouldn't have to wonder if I were doing it behind her back . . .again.

It's no secret that I got it goin' on. My nickname really should be *Black Woman's Wish*, or better yet, *Well-Endowed Black-*

Woman's Wish. Don't get me wrong, I'ma good husband, but at the same time I'ma ladies' man. Which is why Rena has never really trusted me. She's always accused me of sleeping around with other women. I must admit I messed around with a few. However, she never had any proof until the day lil' twenty-two year old Shonda called the house. Trust me, fucking with young girls will do it to you every time.

Rena was in the kitchen preparing dinner for the family when the phone rang.

"Hello," Rena said.

"Speak to Rena?"

"This is she."

"Well, this is Shonda and I'm just callin' to give you my new address."

"What? Who is this and why would you want to give me your new address?"

"So you'll know where your baby daddy, Greg, is when he leaves you for me."

"Baby daddy?" Rena said, almost mumbling. "I don't know who the hell this is but don't call here lying on my man!"

"Please, spare me the baby mama drama. You don't have to believe me, but the next time I'm over your house right after I get out of your king size bed, and need to shower make sure you leave enough lavender liquid soap for me to use."

Rena's eyes widened, as she knew this woman had been in our house, and to make matters worse, used her favorite soap. She had a gut feeling that something was going on behind her back but she never thought that it would go this far.

"You've been in my home?" Rena said in disbelief. "Around my family and in my bed?"

"Yes, girl, and I've even eaten your food. What was that you cooked the other night, Scrimp and Ramen noodles? Oh, that was *delicious*! Also, Boo, where did you get them sheets from? Trust me, you've got great taste in linen. What were those, 1000 thread count sheets on your bed? 'Cause I ain't, feel no beads or nothin' on 'em. Ooooh, the smoothness felt great rubbing against my naked ass!"

"You sick bitch!" Rena screamed, "How dare you call here and tell me this! You must be some young silly ass girl that has a thing for my man!"

"*No*, I don't have a thing *for your* man, we got a thing for *each other*. Besides I'm doing you a favor by telling you, but if you're too stupid to see what's right in your face then that's on you. But since you wanna break bad, just know that when he shows up missin', my address is listed." Shonda hung up.

Rena held the phone in her hand, listening to the dead sound of the dial tone. She was in shock and didn't know what to think. After she hung up the phone, she sat at the kitchen table trying to figure out what had just happened. Thinking back, she knew all along that I was a man you had to keep your eyes on, one that had always been very friendly with the ladies. Charm is my middle name. After all, Denzel looks like *me*. I'm 6'4, with short, black hair, and 225 pounds of solid milk chocolate. I'm also a senior advisor at a major stock brokerage firm who dresses his ass off! I'm always dipped and would have it no other way. You'll never catch me looking bad; my hands are always manicured and my goatee is always tight. I am what most women would define as successful, fine, and irresistible. So, quite honestly I couldn't understand why Rena was trippin' so hard after she got off the phone with Shonda; she knew that some women just couldn't bear to see me be a faithful man.

Rena warned me about my behavior several times prior to Shonda calling. So I knew eventually things would have to change between us. Rena has always loved me with all of her heart but she grew tired of feeling like she was being trampled on. We've been married for eleven years, and for seven out of the eleven, Rena has always found phone numbers in my pants' pockets, not to mention that the phone would ring all times of the night. Every time Rena confronted me, I always told her that the numbers belonged to a new client; and as for the late night phone calls . . .I simply told her that I was going to ask *her* why the phone always rang late at night.

Rena's nosey ass girlfriends all told her that I was cheating on her, however, Rena was the Hillary Clinton type, and stood by her man. She would tell them, "If I didn't see it, then it didn't happen."

Rena may have said one thing, but the look on her face showed that she was miserable. I hated to see my beautiful wife so unhappy; after all, she had it going on too. Trust me, Gregory Robbins would have it no other way. Rena's got a bangin' body, 36-24-46, brick house thick, with mid length, black, kinky twist in her hair. She works out three times a week at the local gym and she ain't doing too bad in the financial department either. She brings home a sizeable income as a Pediatrician. Not to mention that she's given me two beautiful daughters, Kayla 10 and Kalani, 7. Rena can't offer anymore than she already has.

"How could he do this to me!" she was screaming when I came into the house. When I went to see what was wrong, she stopped pacing the floor, stood at the kitchen counter, and started stabbing the cutting board with a large knife. I was scared as hell and I knew instantly that something had to really be wrong. The girls are normally running around the house. The television is normally blasting with the Proud Family cartoon. But on this day all I could hear were the birds chirping as Rena ranted like a crazy woman. Before I could even attempt to ask her what the hell had taken over her body, she stomped upstairs to our bedroom.

"Rena!" I yelled.

"What do you want? I'm upstairs in *my* bedroom."

"*My* bedroom?" I said to myself as I carefully walked toward the bedroom door. Rena was sitting at the vanity and the bed was unmade. All I could think about was Waiting to Exhale and Rena burning my shit, so I kept my distance.

"What's goin' on Baby?" I asked, standing next to the door. "Where are the girls?"

"I sent them to my mother's house."

"Oh, okay."

"Why are you standing in *my* bedroom?" she spat.

"*Your* bedroom?" I said, trying to assert some type of authority in my voice. "Why do you keep saying *your* bedroom? This here *our* juke joint!" I laughed trying to loosen up the tightness in the room with some humor. When I saw she didn't crack a smile I said, "Baby, is there some reason this isn't *our* bedroom anymore?"

"What do you think?!" she screamed.

I really didn't know what she was talking about. She had a blank stare in her eyes and the more I looked at her, the more I thought about breaking the hell out.

Before I could move Rena screamed, "You had that bitch in my house didn't you?"

"What bitch, what the hell are you talkin' about?" I was trying to play dumb, but I knew exactly who she was referring to.

"Shonda!" she screamed.

"I don't know a damn Shonda!" I lied.

"Stop lying to me Greg. She called here today and told me *everything*. She even knew what kind of soap I liked! The bitch used my *soap*, my favorite fuckin' *soap*." Rena started to cry, "Greg, how could you?"

"Rena please," I said, not knowing what else to say.

"Please my ass! I can't believe that you have done this to me again! Why Greg? Why?"

My heart started pounding 'cause I knew I was busted. I had a choice to make and I had to make it fast. Either I took it like a man or I broke the hell out. I decided to take it like a man, stand here, and lie about me knowing this person Rena was screaming about. "Somebody is trippin' Baby," I said as calmly as possible. "I don't know any Shondas. Hell Baby, I don't know a LaShonda, RaShonda, To-Shonda, Tomika or a Lakisha for that matter. You the only woman in my life. Baby, are you sure it wasn't one of your girlfriends playin' a joke on you?" "Don't fuck with me Greg! My friends don't play like that." The hurt in her eyes was ripping me apart. I'd never seen her so upset before. "She told me she ate my food," Rena screamed, "Shrimp, no excuse me she said '*scrimp*' and Ramen noodles? Gregory, come on now. Nobody but you knew that we were doing that. That was *our* little recipe. She called me a 'baby mama.' But what topped it off was that she said I had great taste in linen because my 1000 threat count sheets felt good rubbing against her naked ass." his was gon' be a tough one to work my way out of, so I thought.

"I want you out of here!" Rena demanded, "Pack your shit and get the fuck out! Don't wait to leave me, since that's what your girlfriend called to inform me."

"Leave you?" I said, surprised, as even that one threw me for a loop. "I'm not leaving you, I love you too much!"

"Shut up. You're lying! And since you wanna lie to the bitter end, go to your bitch's house and lie to her, because I'm not hearing it anymore!"

All I could do was stand there for a second and process what Rena had just said to me. Her stare was cold and she didn't even seem to blink. If looks could kill I'd be dead as hell at this point.

"Baby can we please work this out? I admit I had a fling with this girl but it didn't mean anything to me. I'm always here with the kids alone. We need you Baby. You're always putting your job before us." I figured if I flip the script on her she'd start trying to defend herself instead of keeping the blame on me.

"Bullshit! Don't even try to play me. You think I'm stupid? Now you're trying to play on my intelligence? I tell you what, get your shit and get the fuck out! Yo ass got to go!"

Rena wasn't hearing anything I was saying. The more I talked the angrier she became. Everything I said she took it as a lie. I had to play my last trump card "Let's go get counseling Baby." I fell on my knees and started moving toward her, "Baby I need you. If I lose you and the girls, I would die. Please Baby. I'ma sick man. I'ma change. I will. Just don't leave me. What you wanna do? Go to church . . .pray? Come on let's call your mama so she can help us pray. You know how she likes to do that."

"Why do you do this to me Greg?" Rena said looking down at me.

I could see a little sparkle of love in her eye, so I placed my head in her lap and said, "Please, let's work this out. I think counseling would do us some good." After a few minutes the anger started to relinquish in her eyes. I lifted myself off the floor and sat on the edge of the bed. Rena got up and paced around the room as if she were trying to figure out if I was serious or was this just another attempt to try and stay in the house.

"Alright Greg, I tell you what, I'll go to counseling on one condition."

"Anything Baby," I said sounding desperate.

"After we are done with counseling you have to have a open mind about some changes I want to make around here."

"Changes, like what?"

"Just promise me that you'll have an open mind, that's all." I didn't know what I was making a promise to, but to get out of this, I was willing to do anything. "Alright Baby, I'll do you one better. I promise to go along with *any* changes you want around here." That must've hit the spot because her face brightened up completely, as she heard my words.

A little smirk ran across her face as she said, "I'll make the appointment for us as soon as possible. But you have to sleep in the guest room tonight. I don't know when I'll be able to sleep with you again."

I walked out the room a happy but defeated man. I was happy that I still had a place to lay my head and I still had my family. But, I was defeated in knowing that my playa days were over. No more running the streets. No more flirting with women in the grocery store trying to swap phone numbers.

The next morning on my way to work my best friend Darryl and I stopped by Dunkin' Donuts down the street from our office. That's where Shonda worked. Darryl knew I was seeing her and he asked me the same question everyday, "Why are you risking everything you have for a female that makes barely minimum wage?"

My answer was always the same; "Life is made up of risks, and I live life to the fullest." To Darryl that answer never really made sense, but to me it was clear. I knew I was taking a risk sleeping with her but the sex was so good I had to keep coming back for more.

As Darryl and I walked into the doughnut shop, Shonda looked up and saw us coming through the doors. She was at the cash register and when she spotted me she tried to slow down servicing the customer so she wouldn't have to talk to me. But the lady at the register was getting agitated, so Shonda had no choice but to hurry up. As soon as the woman walked away from the cash register, I took her spot in front of Shonda.

"May I help you?" Shonda smirked.

"Yeah, we need to talk now!" I demanded.

"Look Greg," she said sucking her teeth and rolling her eyes, "can't you see I'm at work. This is Dunkin' Donuts and this is the mornin' rush." Then she popped her neck and snapped her fingers.

"Well I tell you what, if you don't talk to me right now, I'm gonna tell everybody where they can get that freaky lil' nasty video you made. Now try me if you think I'm playin' I got a couple copies in the car!"

Shonda shook with anger but she knew I would stand by my words. "I need to take a smoke break, I'll be right back," she said to her manager. She walked out the front door with me following her.

"Why the fuck did you call my house and upset my wife?" I said with my teeth clinched.

"I didn't call your damn house yesterday!"

"I didn't say it was yesterday silly bitch! I ought to knock your ass out for that shit. You almost cost me everything."

"Kiss my ass. I almost cost you everything? Please. I'm not the one callin' and beggin' for some pussy, *you is*," Then she began mocking me, "Shonda, come on over so we can get into somethin' before my wife gets home, she cooked some scrimp and noodles."

"That still gave you no right to call my house!" I said wanting to slap the shit out of her. "And by the way it's shrimp, not scrimp, ya dumb hoe!"

"Please," she said sucking her teeth. "Spare me. Plus, you ain't no good no how and what you doin' is wrong, *fornditation* is a sin."

"*Fornditation*? If you ain't 'bout the dumbest . . .
Its For*ni*cation. And how in the hell are you trying to have morals and you sleeping with a married man? Shut up, cause you don't make no damn sense. But it's all good cause I'm still with my wife, so your little plan didn't work after all!"

"Whatever nigga!" she said tossing her hand in the air, "didn't nobody like your lil' minute man ass anyway. That lil' short ass dick, that's why you only got one ball! Can't bust a nut for shit, what was that, water that shot outta you the last time? She can have yo' Viagra needin' ass. Old motherfucker! You gon' come up to my job, I should shoot yo' ass!"

She had lost her mind. Even Darryl was scared as he yelled, "Greg, come on man!"

"Fuck you bitch!" I spat. Then I jumped in the car.

"You take Viagra man?" Darryl asked.

"Nigga no!"

* * *

A few days after Shonda called the house Rena and I started going to marriage counseling. I figured I'd show up and tell all our marital problems to some balding white guy with 100 college degrees on his wall. He would tell us that we don't have a problem and that would be that and we would go back to our lives and live happily ever after. How wrong was I! I was shocked when we walked into Dr. Pamplin's office. There he stood a 6'3", bald, well dressed, and educated black man. He had to have been in his mid 30's and looked as if he had ran through a few women himself. As he introduced himself to us, I noticed that he was not wearing a wedding ring on his left hand but he was wearing a silver band on his right hand. I passed it off as a fashion trend. The session began with us telling him why we were there in the first place.

"Well my husband has a problem with being faithful to me," Rena jumped right in telling the doctor all about her suspicions and the mess that happened with Shonda. She began to cry as she talked about it. I noticed she even moved away from me on the sofa as she remembered all the things I had done.

"Mrs. Robbins," the doctor said, extending his hand.

"Call me Rena," she said accepting his gesture.

"Okay Rena," the doctor said, after shaking my hand, and then sitting behind his desk. "How did the two of you meet?"

I could tell I was not the only person in the room confused

by the question.

"What does that have to do with anything?" I asked. All I need is for this doctor to start bringing up old memories about some other women I've had. Rena shot me a look as to tell me to shut up.

"In order to figure out *what* went wrong," the doctor stated, "You have to figure out *where* it went wrong Greg."

"Call me Mr. Robbins," I said with a serious attitude. I didn't see the point in pulling up old feelings that were buried years ago. Rena andI have been married for 11 years and have two beautiful little girls, so there was no need in going back in time.

Again Rena jumped in and started talking about how we met.

"We met back in college 13 years ago. He was the Head drum major and I was a dancer for the band. He always had the reputation of being a ladies' man and rumor had it he had been with half the females in the band."

I sat there and listened to my wife tell this stranger all about me.

"We started out as just friends. He was dating this one girl on the squad with me but he was not shy about letting me know that he wanted to be more than friends. He drove a nice car for a college student and had his own apartment. So one day after band practice I saw him," Rena said, as if I were a stranger.

"He and his girlfriend were having an argument," she continued. "They were cursing and going on like an old married couple. Everybody was standing around as the two of them fussed back and forth. In the middle of him taking his turn to curse her she hauled off and slapped him across the face. He surprised me because he just stood there for a second and walked away. I was stuck on him from that point forward. For a man to stand there in front of all of his boys and allow a woman to slap him and he just walks away showed me that he was a man that would never raise his hands to a woman. It also showed me that he's the type of guy that would rather walk away than to stand there and fight. He impressed me."

Dr. Pamplin wrote down everything Rena said. He then

turned his attention to me.

"So, Mr. Robbins is there anything else you would like to add."

"No, That's just about right."

"So Rena you knew he was a ladies man when the two of you met?"

"Yes," she said, seemingly embarrassed, "I knew."

I'm sitting next to Rena wondering where this was going. It was starting to sound like the Doc and I were on the same page.

"Well why marry him if you knew he was a ladies man, charming and all those other words you used to describe him?"

"Well . . .I thought I could change him."

"Why would he do that? What's so special about you that you think you can change a man? Better yet a grown man?"

The more he talked the more I liked him. He was telling her like it is. Everything I wanted to say to her he was doing it for me. I was and am *a ladies* man. I am *charming, smart, well endowed, and overall a* damn good catch! Simply put, women can't resist me. Hell, if I knew marriage counseling would put the truth out there like this, I would've come the first time I had an affair. Pleased with the way things were going, I reared back on the couch and crossed my legs.

Rena rolled her eyes as she continued, "I was raised thinking that if you were married your husband would automatically be faithful."

"That was your second mistake," the doctor added. Visibly annoyed with Rena he said, "You marry a man that you don't trust and then you thought you could change him? And on top of that you try and live by something that your parents, who were married in a different time and era, told you?"

I was smiling from ear to ear. This was working out perfect. As far as I was concerned this doctor was *the niggah,* if it wasn't for sparing Rena's feelings, I would've reached over and gave him a pound and said, "Right on my brotha!"

The doctor wasn't holding anything back. I could tell he was hurting her, but hell, this was something she needed to hear.

Our hour was almost up when the doctor left us with these parting words.

"The two of you are here for two reasons. One, you want to stay married to him and two, you're not gonna change him and that is evident. So what I suggest is you find a way to explore your marriage. If he's not willing to give up women try admiring women with him. Take an interest in what gets him going."

"Rena eyes widened as she listened to him "But doctor…""

"Sorry your time is up. Make an appointment with my secretary on your way out. Have a good day."

I gave the doctor a hug before I left. Rena still tried to speak but the doctor wouldn't let her get another word in. I was satisfied with the session. Rena on the other hand seemed to be fuming mad at what she was just told.

"He wants me to look at other women with you? What kinda shit is that?"

"Annie Mae," I said like Ike Turner, "You gon' have to do what the doctor said do." Hell, I couldn't help but laugh; to me this was like a dream come true. It was like having an actual doctor with a medical degree, write me a prescription to fuck other women and my wife know about it. Hell not since, L.L.'s Rock the Bells, MCM suits, and Gazelles did I feel like this. Humph, at thirty-six, life is great! "Don't knock it Baby," I said. "There are a lot of sexy and classy women out there. Rena, you never know you just might like it."

The car was quiet all the way home I couldn't stop smiling. I looked over at Rena and she looked like she wanted to spit fire. We drove up to the house and she made a beeline to the front door. "I have to call my girl Jennifer and tell her about this shit!" I walked behind her listening to her curse all the way into the house. She went into the bedroom and slammed the door. I just sat on the sofa, turned the television on, slid my hands in my pants, and tried to relax with my doctor's note.

For a minute, I must admit that Dr. Pamplin was kinda unprofessional. The things he told us were not what I would have expected from a well-known and respected counselor. But, he did say everything I wanted him to, and she seems to want to go along with it because the doctor ordered it. Who am I to complain? I'm about to have my cake and eat it too.

Chapter 2

Rena's Eyes

Now what's really funny is Greg's sitting out there thinking that he's the man right now he has no idea about the scam that David, oh excuse me Dr. Pamplin, and I just pulled on him.

"Dr. Pamplin's office please." After a few minutes he picked up the phone. "Hey David," I said. "This is Rena."

"What's up girl? Your man is too gullible," he chuckled.

"I know. He's too busy thinking about all the women he can openly sleep with to realize we just played his ass."

David and I met our sophomore year in college. He was just one of those guys that never wanted anything from you but your friendship. He was always there for me when I needed someone to talk to. Besides it didn't hurt to walk around with one of the sexiest football players at school. I could always be open with my feelings with him and he never judged me no matter how dumb I was being at the time. So when he told me he was gay I never thought about breaking our friendship off because I didn't believe in his lifestyle. He and his partner in college, who also played on the football team, were what we call today under cover brothers. Nobody knew the two of them were lovers except for the crowd they hung around. To look at either of them there was no way you would expect them to be homosexuals.

"Girl," David said, "I'm telling you he'll never expect that you have an interest in women."

"I hope not. I don't know how he'd react if I just jumped out there and said I want to be with another women while you watch. He's the type that feels like if there is fuckin' goin' on he needs to be a part of it."

"Then that's what you do."

"I don't get it. What do you mean?"

"You have to let him be apart of it if you want to get your freak on. If you do it any other way he's liable to flip and act a fool on you."

"So you're sayin' let him lead me to other women?"

"That's exactly what I'm saying."

The more I thought about it the more I liked the idea. Since he is always getting phone numbers and chatting with women on the Internet, I'll allow him to do it openly and I'll reap all the benefits. "I think it'll work," I smirked. "Right now he's on the sofa probably going through all his numbers trying to find the freakiest women he knows."

"Let him call her and set it up. You just keep acting like he has to pressure you into it and then get your freak on."

"Okay, I'll let you know how it turns out." I had to get back into character acting like the wife that is so hurt, before I go back out there and talk to Greg. As I walked into the living room there he was sitting in the recliner with his chest all poked out feeling like the man. I wanted to yell, "You so damn stupid!" but I figured that would not get me what I wanted. "So, what are we gonna do now that the doctor has said I have to try finding women attractive with you."

He sat up in the chair and started to lecture me on what he looks for in a woman.

"The first thing you have to do is understand what is sexy to me. I like a woman that is thick and has a nice round ass that I can hold on to."

"So my ass is too small for you?"

"No, it's okay but I really like those big bubble butts the kind guys make jokes about putting their drink on."

"Okay, what else?"

"I like women that are very busty. The bigger the better."

I looked down at my chest. I could fill up a C cup bra pretty good but I guess that was not good enough for him. Sitting there describing a woman that is the total opposite of me really hurt. It made me feel like I was not good enough for him.

Everything about me was wrong in his eyes but I held my tongue.

"What kind of women do you find attractive?" Greg asked.

For a woman to say that she thinks another women is pretty or attractive is no big deal. So I had no problem telling him.

"I think women that are kinda slender with a well toned body is attractive."

"They are okay, but a thick sistah is gorgeous to me," he insisted.

"Well I think we need to meet somewhere in the middle if we are gonna try this together." I could see the excitement in his eyes as we talked about different women. To be honest that was the best conversation we had in a long time. He went on and on about the type of women that he liked. I don't think he ever thought once about my feelings or if he did he didn't care. All he seemed to think about was getting into another woman and not have to hide it.

"Well," he said, "I know a few women that might be interested in getting with the both of us."

When he said that, I wanted to slap the hell out of him on the spot. How dare he offer me a woman that he has probably already been with in my bed and introduce her to me so they can do it again in my bed this time with me.

"Before we go any further I think we need to set some ground rules," I said.

He instantly deflated. You could see the life fall out of him as he waited for me to finish. "I don't want to be with anyone you've already been with or talked to. I want this to be new for both of us." I felt like if I'm gonna sleep with another woman I'm gonna at least have some say in who she is. "Second," I continued, "we will not be with any of our current friends." I don't know if I could ever look one of our friends in the face after sleeping with them. I think that would just make for a very odd situation. "And last, we will only look for single bisexual women. I don't want to get caught up in no drama with some woman that's cheating on her man. And she must be professional like us and very, very, very discrete; the last thing I want is for my personal life to be all over the streets. I could lose my practice if the public found out I was into sleeping with other women with my man."

He sat looking at me trying to process all of what I'd said. I knew he wouldn't have a problem with it. It gives him the opportunity to find new women.

"I can agree with all of your demands. Not a problem," he said easily, trying to hide his smile.

For the first time I cracked a little smile. It was finally going to happen. I would have my first taste of a woman. I'd heard that only a woman can really perform oral sex on another woman correctly. I wanted to find out for myself. I must admit I'm already a little nervous. I've never been with another woman before, but I've often fantasized about it. But even bigger than that, how do you ask another women to sleep with you and your man? How do you find this person? I guess I'd better ask the pro himself how he goes about meeting women.

"So, how are we gonna find a woman that is willing to sleep with both of us?" I figured if anybody knew; it was him.

"Well I've heard that the Internet is a good place to look for whatever it is you are into."

Now he's gonna sit here and act like he's never been on the net looking for and talking to women. Okay, I'ma play his little game.

"Well, I guess we can put an ad on one of those sites?" I asked innocently.

"Yeah I know a couple sites we can put an ad on that are made just for swingers and people looking for bisexual people." He got up and walked into the den where the computer is. "Can we look now?" He was so happy as he turned on the computer and typed in the sites he wanted to go to. He could have at least acted like he had to think about the names of the sites. I pulled up a chair next to him and watched as he hopped from web site to web site looking for the right one for him . . .I mean us. "What do you think about this site Baby?"

The name of the site was BiBlackSingles.com. I figured that this was a good place to start. We put in our information and the information of what we were looking for. I noticed on the site where it asks, "are you a couple or single?" He put in "single"; I guess out of habit. He quickly changed it hoping I didn't see that.

When it asked us to describe the person that we desired he put in "She has to be thick in all the right places. Very busty. A good head on her shoulders and drama free." Since I was going to be with her to I had him add that "she had to be drug and disease free and always practice safe sex. And, she must be very discrete and professional. No hoochies." I guess these things were not important to him but to me, it was a must.

After the site accepted us, we looked at a few of the pictures of women who were members already of the web site. I must admit some were women that could get any man under the sun. I even recognized some of them. I had no idea that so many women were on looking for the same thing that I was. All of the women that fit our profile were women that had great jobs and well respected, but had a freaky side. These were the types of women that I found attractive. Greg was more interested in the young hoochies that were cheating on their man or baby daddy. After looking at all the ads that were in our profile we decided to contact this one lady named Lisa. She was from the same city as us in just another zip code. Her ad read: *"I'm looking for a couple or single bi female to become friends with first and let nature take its course. The people I contact must be discrete and drug and disease free with no drama. I'm into outside concerts, dining out, and I collect DVD's. I'm attracted to athletically build people, mid 30's, African American and if you drink that's okay. Hope to hear from you soon."*

At the end of the ad, she had a picture of herself. She was drop dead gorgeous. Her lips were full and her skin was flawless. She had large round breast and filled up a pair of jeans nicely. I was instantly attracted to her and her ad sounded perfect to me. I had Greg send her an e-mail letting her know that we were interested in getting to know her. We looked at a couple other people on the site, but none grabbed my attention like Lisa. Greg was like a kid in a candy store. He wanted to send an e-mail to every woman on the site.

"Why don't we e-mail her?"

"No, she's ghetto."

"What about her?" Greg said.

"No, she's way beyond thick."

He jumped all over that site trying to find anything. I had my mind set on Lisa. I told Greg that one e-mail was enough for me for one day. Of course he felt like we should flood the Internet with our profile but I had to play my game. Besides I had a feeling that Lisa would be contacting us very soon. Greg got up to get a cup of water. While he was away, I sent her a picture of me on vacation that was still on our digital camera. The picture was of me standing on the beach in a two-piece white bikini. Not to brag, but I was looking damn good in the picture, and I was sure she'd think the same thing.

Other Titles by
Two of A Kind Publishing

Swingers
by Torrian Ferguson

Little Ghetto Girl
by Danielle Santiago

Cha-Ching
by Tonya Blount

To order visit
www.twoofakindpublishing.com

Attention Writers

Two of a Kind Publishing is currently seeking new authors of urban fiction including poetry, testimonies and autobiographies.

Submission Guidelines

- Synopsis and first four chapters required
- Typed, double-space, 1 ½ inch margins all around and only on one side of the page
- 12-point font in Times New Roman
- Cover letter stating address, phone number, the type of work being submitted
- A photo of author

No manuscripts will be returned. Please include a self-addressed, stamped envelope for a prompt response.

All manuscripts should be addressed to:

Two of a Kind Publishing
Attn: Submissions
3120 Milton Road Ste
Charlotte, NC 28215

*Check us out on the web for information on our latest publications
and featured authors at
www.twoofakindpublishing.com*